"This graceful, lyrical, and del
fellow human who seeks solac
Penn May goes deeper and d
the reader experiences confusion, fear, hope, and love along with him, and May is brave enough to tackle and illuminate the big mysteries: how and why we keep going, how we face death, how we connect or fail to, how we hide from our desires, and how we accept the inevitable."

Mary Troy, award-winning author
The Alibi Café, *Beauties*, and *Swimming on Highway N*

"I really enjoyed *Margery*... an almost surreal atmosphere...stirs up all sorts of emotions: despair, sorrow, a sense of reality, irony, tension, grief, courage, love, anger, hope."

Carol Cole, editor

"A lone hiker is drawn deep into the woods and emerges into a community set apart from the real world. What unfolds for him there—and the secret he discovers—isn't what you might expect. With its rich descriptions of the natural world, its wise and articulate insights, its cast of humane characters, *Margery* addresses the deepest and most important issues we face. It's Jeffrey Penn May's best book."

John Dalton, prize-winning author
Heaven Lake and *The Inverted Forest*

"Literary and thought-provoking; it's something I think we all experience in different ways, a search for meaning, if you will."

Mary Ward Menke, editor

"A bizarre journey."

John Reichle, Outdoor Education Specialist

"The characters, and situations on the trail, have these small moments, words and gestures that feel fresh. *Margery* by Jeffrey Penn May is clever and has great plot points, but mainly I see the characters' positive quirks in people I encounter throughout my day."

Julie Heller, Outdoor Enthusiast

Margery

Jeffrey Penn May

Copyright © 2023 by Jeffrey Penn May

All rights reserved.

No part of this book may be reproduced or transmitted in any form or by any means, electronic or mechanical, except for the purpose of review and/or reference, without explicit permission in writing from the publisher.

Cover design copyright © 2023 by Niki Lenhart
nikilen-designs.com

Published by Paper Angel Press
paperangelpress.com

ISBN 978-1-959804-46-8 (Trade Paperback)

10 9 8 7 6 5 4 3 2 1

FIRST EDITION

ACKNOWLEDGMENTS

Thank you to my brothers, my parents, cousins, aunts and uncles, to those long gone in prairie dust, mountain summits, cool clear streams … to my grown children connecting to the future and my wife who once again sustained me with her life-saving research.

To family and friends, their intriguing and humorous ideas whirring from the lighting of a backpacking stove, from the flames of campfires, and from long hikes, fictional characters coming alive from a process still a mystery.

To readers and editors who understand that these characters have their own life, independent of mine, and helped me avoid messing it up too much.

Thanks to Paper Angel Press for their promptness, professionalism, and good humor.

1

AS I HIKED FURTHER INTO THE WOODS, deeper than I'd ever gone before, I noticed darkness not only surrounding me from the thick canopy of hardwood trees, their leaves abnormally large, but also felt a heaviness in my heart, a tightness in my chest that was counter to all my previous experiences hiking into the wilderness.

Usually I felt exultant at the blood and oxygen and endorphins rushing through my body, making me thank God, nature, pure existence. But not this time as I forged along this narrow winding path, an innocent offshoot to the heavily used trail, a path that begged for exploring, one that reasonable people should be turning away from … but I've always felt drawn to the unknown, to the receding view around the bend. Sometimes I went too far, and this time I followed the path through underbrush, nothing more than the hint of a trail, and came upon a shallow clear stream about a dozen strides wide, roots of trees tangled along the banks.

I stopped and sat, backpack against a tree, my feet dangling from a root wad, feeling exhausted, almost crushed by the effort of moving. Not like me at all. What was going on? Should I sleep here, or retreat?

Margery

Should I try to lay out my one-person tent along the small, twisting snake of a footpath and sleep? Darkness was seeping in around me and I suddenly felt more alone, more apprehensive than ever before.

In that moment, I chose to reflect; or more likely, I had no choice—my nature has always tended toward too much reflection. I was raised in middle-class privilege that has been eroding for many years, slowly at first but accelerating with each passing year and with the acceleration, my way of connecting with the world and with myself had regressed. I longed for an earlier time, a time when I could conquer whatever lay ahead, a time when I knew less, but was confident I knew a lot—I pretended to be a smart man and practiced formal English until it became a habit, and was often accused of being old-fashioned, but as I aged, it felt natural to speak and think like those long dead. I'm not hip, not cutting edge or fashionable, my style perpetually retro, wardrobe waiting to become trendy again because there is of course nothing new under the sun—except the progressive cascading swell of technology, but my phone was dead and gladly buried at the bottom of my backpack.

The other side of the stream was even more dense with tree roots than where I sat and squinted, looking to see if the path continued, but couldn't tell, couldn't make out any passage through heavily leafed thickets and thorns. I looked over my shoulder at the path I'd taken—a narrow tube-like passage—and wondered how I'd managed this far, ending up here, which was nowhere. My bare legs were scraped, but that was to be expected, hiking in shorts when paths like this one were more suited to long pants. My hands had thin scrapes with blood dotting along the wounds, but the wounds were minor. I had no idea how it happened. Normally, I wouldn't notice such things … so that was normal. I shut my eyes to listen—the forest sounds sometimes soothing—and heard a twig snap, an unnatural sound from across the shallow stream.

A young man, perhaps in his twenties, splashed into the water and stood staring at me, eyes brilliantly blue, jaw sharp with a short dark-brown beard, wearing ragged blue jeans, and a T-shirt with no brand names, no logos or witty quotes, nothing, just plain black, worn and dirty—a younger version of me—and he stood barefoot, water rising up to his ankles, soaking his jeans, his long dark hair tangled. If I'd seen him on the streets, I'd have thought him homeless, but here, he might be with a group of backpackers trekking into the unknown—and my thoughts seemed confirmed by his nonchalant greeting.

"Hey, how's it going?" He turned away, grabbing a tree root and pulling himself out on the opposite bank.

"Wait!" I called, "Where does this path lead?"

"Here," he replied. "It leads here."

He might have said something more, or it could have been just a splash, a rustle of leaves, or maybe the wind, and he disappeared through the brush, rising up the slope, again ignoring my calls to wait, so I took off my boots, waded across, nearly falling while climbing the root wads on the other side. I sat in the midst of a bramble and pulled my socks and boots back on over wet feet—my feet would dry and everything would be fine.

The evening was settling in, making the already shrouded forest darker and more difficult. *Where'd that guy go?* I hiked up the incline through the underbrush and soon my backpack got caught on a branch, and I tangled myself in a thicket and cussed and thought about shouting for help, but I'd done that only once in my life, pinned in the twisted wreckage of a car, and even then I could have gotten out on my own, so maybe it was pride keeping me from calling for help now.

I'd always been able to enter the forest and return in better spirits than when I'd started, but now I felt like giving up. Normally, I'd gut it through okay and break free of the bramble and go along my way, a better person for the struggle, but I felt trapped, worn out, noticing the stark contrast to the vitality of the young man who'd bounded away into the dense forest, apparently so "one" with his surroundings that he could melt through impenetrable underbrush.

My arms and hands had new gouges, not deep punctures but enough for me to smear the blood a few times before it dried. I stared at the dried blood, and the age spots patterned along the back of my hand like a map, as if they would lead me out of this mess, and lunged forward, pulling my tangled leg free, and pushed mightily against a branch. After a series of maneuvers, twisting my limbs so much that the pain lingered, I fell onto a narrow, barely noticeable V-shape in the undergrowth. I stepped carefully in the direction of what sounded like muffled voices, but couldn't be sure; my mind starting to trick me, the voices like a memory, hallucinations from the past seeping into my immediate future. Somewhere in the darkening forest ahead there was the crackling of a campfire, and a glimmer of hope appeared in the blackness, a flame, and then the glowing blue dome of a tent, making me think of spaceships, and aliens settled into our world. The young man was hunched over the fire, warming his hands near the flames. I stumbled into the campsite.

"What took you so long?" He sounded tired, but vigorous, his voice edgy.

I nodded up the slope, the earth rising above us in the dark. "Had to explore the ridgeline first."

He glanced at me, and I could see the moment he thought it possible I had climbed higher and explored the ridge in the impossibly short time since meeting him at the stream. We exchanged a few words in which he claimed he had told me to follow him, but obviously I didn't hear—my hearing not a subject I wanted to talk about—so we fell into a natural silence. As I wondered who this homeless backpacker was, youthful and vibrant and alive, he mumbled something else I didn't hear. He grimaced, then smiled—must've been something sardonic and funny—white teeth set against the layer of earth coating his windblown face, while I stood tired and uneasy, my teeth yellow from smiling at too many sunsets, and from inhaling the rust-colored clouds wafting up and swirling around glass, gem-studded lights in the lowlands, where the bleating noises of civilization overpowered my cries for solitude.

It was almost night, the light coming from the campfire, and I had been standing there for what seemed like forever, as everything sometimes did in the orange glow of crackling campfires. In the faint grayness of the descending light, the woods rustled and a young woman appeared from the dark and stood at the young man's side, wearing jeans and a T-shirt like his, and my gaze fell upon her small breasts, perfectly round, small nipples, enough to make me uncomfortable about my daughter, who lived far away and whom I hadn't seen in so long—this young woman perhaps even younger than my daughter exuding a timeless sexuality, one that I could welcome only for a moment without feeling creepy, or grotesque.

"Hello," she said, as if expecting me, a guest to this camp so far into the woods that for a moment I'd forgotten how I'd gotten there, and then wondered if I'd stumbled into a modern-day fairy tale—or dream—or nightmare in the long tradition of Grimm—my literary sensibilities interfering as they have in the past, barging into my reality and occasionally destroying the perfection of the moment.

I felt wobbly and needed to sit, so I gave in to the weight of my backpack pulling me to the floor of this hardwood forest and leaned heavily against a tree. The young couple watched me with interest but without alarm, as if I were a harmless and nameless woodland mammal settling into a burrow.

My legs felt like slabs of concrete—how long had I been hiking? It wasn't the first time I'd hiked past sunset and searched for a camp, pitching a tent in the dark. But I tried to avoid it, and now a succession of events had piled up on me and made my current hike feel like an impossible slog—odd because I have stood triumphant on mountaintops—but now my arms felt glued to the straps of my pack and I could barely move, and after sliding out of them, I hoped to feel the lightness that comes from releasing heavy burdens, the lightness that always came in the past, the sudden feeling of freedom—releasing the backpack and roaming around the woods like a newborn fawn—but now I struggled to my feet and, while feeling momentarily free, it passed quickly, the weight returning all too soon, a momentary respite but none of the lightness of the past.

I stood across the fire from the two young people, who seemed to be patiently waiting for me. Waiting for what, I wasn't sure, but nonetheless waiting—like I could tell them something useful. We stood across from one another, the fire providing an air of mysticism, as fires always do, and perhaps always have across generations, centuries, millennia.

I studied the young woman, envious not of the young man, whom I assumed was her boyfriend, but that I was not as young as she seemed to be. Yes, I could hike into the dark, could hike for miles, for days, forever and survive, or so I thought, but the exhilaration from the effort was becoming increasingly elusive. She would have no such problem. Though not beautiful in any sort of commercial sense, she was immensely attractive, with athletic hips, and eyes that glistened orange from the fire, but I suspected they must be dark brown and not as reflective as my own blue eyes, which seemed to have been gradually turning gray. Her lips were full and her skin smooth. I would have traded places with her. As if that were possible. I wanted to say something, but what? Conversation silenced by fatigue—or maybe solemnity or laconic demeanor—no one spoke for such a long time that the first words would inevitably be banal. So I kept quiet—clearly among the three of us, I was supposed to be the one with answers, but I had long ago learned that keeping my mouth shut was usually the best approach.

Eventually, I would pitch my small tent, nothing more than a bivouac really, near the fire and would stand there by myself, wondering why I had not been more inquisitive. I thought about saying something but was surprised at my level of exhaustion, so much so that I could barely clear my throat—going for long periods without speaking makes me less inclined to do so. I don't know about you. Maybe it has the opposite effect. There was a time not all that long ago when I would check the statistics, the data, the reports from everyone around the world, check all the sociologically conflicting surveys asking oh-so-important window-to-the-human-soul questions—are you more or less likely to speak after long periods of not speaking at all? While watching the young couple silently staring into the fire, I recalled a *Twilight Zone* episode in which a man bets another man, who was known for his inability to shut the hell up, one million dollars that he couldn't stop speaking for one year, and after the year, the man had lost his ability to utter even a single word. Seems ridiculous, but in the *Twilight Zone* anything is possible—just as it is standing next to a fire, sorting through the details of a fictional world, uneasy about my lapse into silence, afraid I might not recover.

"You hungry?" the young man asked, his voice strong and clear, and his demeanor reminding me of a hippie I'd picked up from the highway a very long time ago while driving from Denver to Portland.

"No," I said hoarsely, "thanks," although I would have gladly eaten a camper's gourmet meal like the kind given on eco-tours.

He shrugged. "We're going to put out the fire –"

The young woman interrupted. "If it's okay with you."

"Yeah," the young man said, "if you need the light ... just put it out when you're finished."

The young woman stepped toward me, extended her hand to shake, a formal greeting that seemed at odds with the environment, as if she were struggling to maintain structure, control of her circumstances. "My name's Kaylee," she said, gripping my hand.

"I'm ..." but I hesitated, holding onto her hand, maybe her vigor, longer than I should while thinking about giving them a false name because mine has always caused me undue consternation. I'm terrible with names, yet they often seem to define us—Kaylee? My awkward silence filled the air with tension—or was it merely my anxiety? She squeezed my hand tighter and let go. Was she trying to reassure me? "Jerome," I said, using my formal name, but quickly steered them away from using Jerry, a comedic name associated with cartoons and sitcoms. "Call me Jeremy," I said, resisting the temptation to say, "Call me Ishmael" and Kaylee released my hand, and I felt as if I'd misplaced something that was just in my grasp a moment ago. Then as I shook the young man's hand, I felt further need to explain myself, "'Jeremy' just sounds better ..."

"Works for me," the young man said, his name easy enough, Josh, and they climbed into their tent, their shadows on the blue dome. I stood watching for awhile, feeling voyeuristic, until their light went out, and I unrolled my tent in the firelight and soon had everything in order, my water bottle, my flashlight, what little remaining food I had hanging from a tree, then kicked dirt into the fire and plummeted into black night. I couldn't see anything, but heard Josh and Kaylee move, or at least thought so, as my hearing seemed lately to be accompanied by a constant humming and ringing. The blackness stayed with me, causing some uneasiness until my eyes finally adjusted to the glow of the evening stars, a half-moon rising from the eastern forest, the chirping of insects ... or was it my brain?

I crawled into my coffin-sized tent, and the ground was hard, my sleeping pad ill-suited for the rocks beneath it, and my thoughts were tinged with a rawness unlike what I'd come to expect here, where I used to find peace. I resisted sleep, perhaps because of what I'd become, or made myself to be; not necessarily horrible, just that there was no going back, no

Margery

starting over, and perhaps it was that cold gray reality continually seeping into my consciousness I didn't want to face in the morning.

    I drifted in and out of sleep, tossing and turning and struggling with my sleeping bag, zipping and unzipping, cold then hot, then cold, mumbling and mangling Robert Frost –*I've tasted desire ... enough of hate ... ice is great ....* And I peeked out the mesh opening to my tent, catching glimpses of the stars past the treetops, finally giving up and rummaging around for my small medical emergency kit, finding a pill and nibbling from the end like the harmless woodland mammal they likely thought I was, giving in to pharmacology and blacking out— regaining consciousness to the smell of dampness, burnt wood and sweat, and the hot brightness of late morning.

2

PUSHING OUT OF MY SLEEPING BAG and struggling out of my small tent, I stood in the fresh cool air and pulled on my shorts, and … the camp was empty. Had they left me? I felt a twinge of embarrassment—maybe Kaylee had suspected something inappropriate in my attraction to her—maybe they were uneasy about me joining them—and then I felt embarrassed at my late waking. Usually I woke early and made coffee.

The fire was smoldering and before I had time to overanalyze my suspicions about why they might abandon me, I saw their backpacks balanced against each other, ready to go, except for one flap not yet secured.

I hastily rolled up my tent and pack. My legs and back hurt, maybe from the hard ground, but probably more because I was no longer young like those two who I now couldn't help but envy as they approached from the woods, hair wet, freshly bathed from the stream. They were content and oblivious—not knowing what disasters might lie ahead—or did they? Did I understand at their age? Could I remember accurately?

They stopped and stared at me as if they'd forgotten I existed.

"Morning," I said. "Must've overslept."

Margery

They greeted me politely, and then Josh shoved his dirty clothes into his pack and tied the flap down. Instinctively I brushed dirt from my shorts that I'd been hiking in for days. How long had I been out in the woods? I'd lost count, maybe close to a week.

"Where you two headed?" I asked, and waited for an invitation to join them.

"Nowhere special," Josh said.

"Me neither." I was trying hard to be light-hearted, and likely it showed.

Kaylee glanced at Josh, then stared at me, her brown eyes unflinching. "Would you like to join us?" she asked. "We're headed home."

"It's over the ridge," Josh said. "I'm surprised you didn't see it yesterday. You know, when you were exploring."

We had an opportunity to share the joke. Nobody in their right mind would have hiked to the ridgeline in the dark.

"No," I said. "Must've missed it."

Kaylee explained that it was a very small town, but I would be welcome and could re-supply and rest. So I followed them on a narrow footpath through dense forest rising into sparse woods matted with pine needles, hiking past rock glades, the steep incline going higher, leading to a place I'd never been before. Once, several years back, while hiking nearby on a trail heading the opposite direction, I'd noticed this ridge rising like the back of a whale, and checked its elevation on the map: not particularly high, with no noticeable summit, but the misty clouds drifting over it and the steeper mountains emerging beyond and rolling on forever made it alluring.

Josh and Kaylee hiked steadily, without resting, their gaits smooth and strong, except that Kaylee slowed occasionally, rolled her shoulders, and rubbed the back of her neck as if she had a headache. I would have asked if she were okay except that I had to focus on keeping pace, my muscles tight and sore, taking deliberate steps designed to conserve energy, and breathing to maximize oxygen, techniques I'd used effectively climbing lots of hills, ridges, and high peaks. In such a way, I could keep up with them.

We finally stopped for a rest in a clearing where the footpath veered to the right and started downhill. Kaylee's face appeared ashen, in contrast to her strong gait, and Josh attended to her with concern while I stood, peering through the woods looking for their home.

Past the trunks of tall, thick pine, it appeared there was a natural carved-out area, a basin, where I could barely glimpse the tops of one or two houses. Josh stepped up next to me. "This way," he said. "You can see better." He surged down the path, and Kaylee brushed past, following him. I lagged behind, but not for long as I joined them standing on a massive rock slab with an open view of their town, a cool breeze wafting up from below, the town nothing more than a group of houses arranged in neat rows situated in the small basin with a stream at the western end cutting into the base of a cliff and flowing south, joining a smaller stream, presumably the one I'd crossed the day before, and churning together to form a river cascading and tumbling down through a narrow gorge to the lowlands from which I'd come. Beyond the cliff, a few jagged peaks with snow fields rising sharply into a pale blue sky, white fingers reaching for the heavens.

The view was astonishing, the breeze like a soft caress, the pine forest below sparse and inviting, and I immediately thought of the novel *Lost Horizon*, not remembering much about it, but associating it with cynicism, perhaps because there is no Shangri-La, and now I thought of my life as a poorly revised account of someone else's life. But this is my story, and it is absolutely true; perhaps nothing more than a blip of time enmeshing my paltry life with yours, but true nonetheless.

"Isn't it beautiful?" Kaylee said, her voice cracking, and maybe a tear on her cheek—might have been sweat.

"Yes," I said, partly out of politeness—it wasn't as though I had never seen beauty in nature.

Josh glanced at me, then hugged Kaylee, and I thought I heard him mutter something like *don't know if I can,* or something similar, my hearing not as acute as I imagined theirs to be, and once again I had a twinge of envy at this young couple so frivolously yet intimately discussing something probably as simple as a dinner invitation or a party, and fleetingly wished I was one of them—either one—her or him or in between—alive and young and temporarily free from the tyranny of what inevitably lay ahead.

Josh led us to the far end of the sloping rock slab where it almost touched the earth and he jumped, then turned and waited for Kaylee as she leapt, and they hugged—or had she stumbled into his arms?—both turning to head down the footpath which expanded into a trail. I climbed carefully over the edge of the rock, sliding to the ground, and watched them holding hands while hiking down the trail, and enjoyed keeping up with them, letting my legs fall easily one in front of the other, happily energetic, never sure where my sudden bursts of energy came from, but grateful they did.

The trail widened, taking us through tall, straight pine and opening to a clearing and emerging onto a road, a two-track that changed to dirt, then gravel, the road taking us past houses on both sides, rustic log cabins, small houses with faded siding and metal roofs, spaced far apart and blending in with the pine forest, and we came to a crossroads. The houses on each corner were slightly larger, each a blend of old and new, septic tanks silver and green and yellow, and pitched roofs.

Josh and Kaylee stopped at the corner, faced each other, and embraced for such a long time, it made me uncomfortable. Finally, Josh turned back toward me, barely slowing as he passed. "See ya," he said.

I expected Kaylee to follow him, but she stayed with me, and watched him go, her face resigned, calm, mature beyond her years. She smiled, but it seemed wistful.

Maybe they'd broken up after a long relationship, and my immediate reaction was that they'd both get over it. And now that she was alone, I felt a confusing attraction, one that made me want to climb mountains with her, feeling simultaneously alive and guilty, as if any attention paid to her would be misconstrued. "You okay?" I asked, and she looked at me directly, and I took a hard look at her for the first time, not the furtive looks from the trail, her thighs swaying, her gait, her rounded shoulders, but her totality, her face in particular, her brown eyes now offering depth and compassion, smooth youthful skin, short curving nose, vaguely imperfect teeth, slight darkness under her eyes as if she hadn't slept.

Her beauty came mostly from within, and her youth drew me in, and I resisted, because the lust of older men stems not because we fall in love, at least in any conventional sense, but because we are cowards about death and refuse to give up our prowess, imagined or otherwise, and lying in the embrace of a young woman is our ridiculous attempt to embrace our own youth.

The sky had become a brilliant blue, dry breeze in green leaves, the pine whispering, the road lined with houses disappearing into the forest patterned against the glistening auburn-striated cliffs. Down the crossroad, the view to the south revealed the V of the gorge where the streams converged, and to the north the encompassing elevation of the basin.

Kaylee touched my arm. "Come on," she said, "I'll show you around."

She turned, headed west toward the cliffs, and we hiked, side by side as if I belonged—the two of us backpacking and now returning from the wilderness.

We met a woman shuffling along with hiking poles, diminutive, stooped, and wearing bright orange running shoes, and Kaylee stopped to chat with her. We exchanged introductions and pleasantries, but I've long since forgotten her name; however, I do remember that the woman was headed for a walk along the ridge and, as we parted, said something curious, "Might go all the way this time." I never saw her again.

The town, if you could call it that, set against the cliff, ridges, forestland surrounding it, was the only sign of human life in this patch of wilderness. Many of the cabins and small homes were deserted, underbrush growing past windows, old shingles slipping from the pitched roofs, many with those old prototype solar panels cracked and faded, tilted, ready to slide to the ground and shatter.

We approached a group of day hikers headed toward the ridge, talking and gesturing, most with walking poles, most of them my age or older. Kaylee stopped and we were suddenly engulfed in social chaos. It made me uncomfortable, made worse when I kept glancing at Kaylee, imagining her as an older woman with me replacing Josh as her boyfriend. There were no children, except a girl probably about fifteen or sixteen; there was an engineer, a pharmacist, a teacher, a plumber and an electrician and a pilot, all of them gregariously willing to reveal every detail about their lives, clearly a group leaning heavily toward extroversion. Thankfully, one of them led the crowd away before I might have been forced to tell my story, which I preferred to keep to myself, as I might blurt out something irrelevant and bizarre or proclaim desire for an imaginary older Kaylee. Not that I haven't exclaimed foolish things before, or that it would particularly bother me all that much, but it was something best avoided.

Margery

I was relieved when they'd gone, but then a man veered around the corner, leading with his big belly tight against his threadbare neoprene top, and nearly toppling over, yellow bandanna tight over what appeared to be a bald head, an outfit suitable for a cheesy gym. He was younger but not quite as fit, walking fast and sweating profusely. Kaylee waved at him and said "hey" and the guy puffed an unintelligible response and continued past us, breathing heavily, maybe to catch up with the others, but he looked like someone who wanted to be left alone, at least while exercising.

As we walked, my mind automatically clicked through practicalities of survival and technology. I considered their source of water, their electricity, all the technical things that could consume me if I let them—the town itself appearing to be virtually energy independent, but I didn't want to know how, didn't want to know the maintenance structure, or the social organization, the who's in charge questions—but yes, there had to be some sort of order, with so many jovial inhabitants. What about the population count? How many? She had implied that the town was sparsely populated, but now I wasn't so sure. Maybe I was missing something.

Kaylee seemed to know what I was thinking. "Relax. You've met almost everyone."

At the western end of the road, she pointed to a small house with red and yellow flowers lining the front porch—the porch common to almost all the houses—yellowing aspen and tall pines providing cool shade. "I live here," she said while slipping off her pack and leaning it against the railing. "You can stay with me if you like." She was gazing into the woods, maybe she'd noticed my furtive glances. The invitation sounded as if it took effort, a tired, what-the-hell, why-not quality to it. After what must have been a long awkward silence while I tried to formulate an answer, she said, "Come on, I'll show you a good place to camp."

Initially, I thought I'd missed an opportunity, but it quickly changed to relief—I wouldn't have to endure inevitably tense, and inevitably exhausting interactions trying to figure out what exactly she wanted.

But then she took my hand, as if to say whatever she had in mind wasn't over, or at least that was my interpretation. Maybe she was just being friendly. Her hand was ice cold. Strange since the late afternoon sun was warm, downright hot if you stood in it long enough.

She led me past another house and then onto a wide trail where she released me and stopped abruptly. She gazed up at the cliff, a tiny waterfall with mist rising out of the forest glistening on the rock face, brown and reddish. She pointed to the top. "Watch!" she urged.

I squinted, searching carefully along the cliff edge, and saw movement, maybe an animal of some sort. I rubbed my eyes, blinked, my sight foggy from not enough sleep, and eventually focused on something blue, maybe some orange or red blended in, clearly a person standing at the edge, possibly looking back at us—at me in particular—daring me to stand on the edge of such a cliff. Ah, I thought, I'd done that before, many times, standing on the edge of a precipice and feeling the pull of gravity. But I'd never done what this person did next, leaping, hurtling through the air, arms outstretched soaring into the treetops, and gone, only to fly back up into the air perilously close to the rock wall and then behind the trees again.

"Wow," I said, studying the cliff, concluding that it was a bungee jump, also concluding that there was nothing safe about it—rock bulging out near the top, sharp ledges, little room for error, the bungee cord blending into the striated cliff, probably slowly being serrated by sharp rocks. "That guy's crazy!"

Kaylee peered at me. "She's done it more than a few times already."

"Okay," I responded, "doesn't make her *not* crazy. Who is she?"

"Margery." The "g" was soft.

"How does she get down, or off, or whatever she does?"

"She drops into the stream. We can go find her if you like."

"Margery?"

3

WE HIKED ONLY A COUPLE MINUTES before emerging into a small clearing next to the stream—wider than the one on the other side of the ridge, and deeper, but you could still see through the crystal-clear water to the bottom, which was lined with smooth tan and white stones, downstream curving into the forest, and upstream framed by trees, huge boulders and crashing white water. The sound of the water, while loud, wasn't overbearing, and for a moment I felt at peace, standing in the shadow of that cliff, shadows creeping toward the town, the day slipping away at an alarming rate.

Margery emerged from the downstream woods, wet hair short and gray-brown, lithe, muscular body, her soaked shoes leaving footprints, a blue T-shirt clearly revealing her small, slightly sagging breasts. And, in my thinking, aroused, but that was just male fantasy—women proudly showing off perpetually aroused nipples—or even more egotistic, maybe she took one look at me and felt the same sort of immediate attraction I felt while gawking at her. Couldn't be that she was merely wet and cold.

Without saying a word, Margery filled the clearing with her presence. She was assessing me methodically, her blue eyes carefully taking note—of

Margery

what exactly I couldn't know, maybe my backpack, which was becoming heavier with each passing moment—Kaylee introduced us, succinctly explaining the circumstance of our meeting, then looked at me and managed a tired, closed smile, momentarily reengaging my desire to possess her youth, to be her, or to connect with her in some way that didn't feel like a perversion.

Margery shifted her stance, almost imperceptibly; a small squish of her wet shoe and she was facing me and in a position to protect Kaylee if needed.

"I was looking for a place to camp," I said, like I needed to explain, but only serving to make me sound guilty.

Kaylee touched my arm and kissed me on the cheek. "See you later," she said, and started walking back, presumably to her blue home.

Margery pulled her shirt away from her chest, twisted the fabric and squeezed, moisture dripping out, then she gestured with a nod—maybe she'd lost her ability to speak—and apparently I was supposed to follow her. To say I was enthralled by her gait and her presence would be an understatement—strong bare legs, muscles defining big veins, smooth silky strides—following along the stream where Margery had hurled herself off the cliff, splashing into the stream. What if the cord snapped? What then? The thought made my muscles twist tight. Only a minute later, and we were in another clearing, smaller, whitewater crashing over the boulders, and beyond that, the upstream twisting up through the trees.

She stopped next to a circle of stones obviously used for campfires. She stared at me, and at first I averted my gaze but then met her eyes for what felt like a significant engagement—we were, I thought, both mature enough to think past naïve apprehension—and in a single gaze we moved energetically past mere acceptance and into intimate connection—faster than our former selves may have ever allowed. Or maybe I was full of shit. Maybe Margery felt sorry for me. Or something else, but none of those mental contortions made any difference.

She moved toward me, and I almost raised my arms to embrace her, but she was merely brushing past to get away. From me, no doubt. However, thinking rationally, she might have just wanted dry clothes. But I needed to hear her voice. "Wait," I said, anticipating a conversation with her filling the space just as her presence had filled the clearing earlier, wanting to hear my name on her lips. I slid my pack off and leaned it against a rock, biding time, watching her begin to formulate her thoughts—

Suddenly, behind me, a branch broke, and someone crashed through the brush. A man, wearing ragged shorts and long sleeve flannel shirt, tattered high-top black boots looking unusually large on skinny hairless legs—he stumbled, went wobbly and managed to stay upright with his walking poles—his skin was flushed and paper thin, yet with his graying hair thick and long, wavy, almost curly, he appeared robust in an odd way. There was something about the shape of his head that wasn't right, face sweating, an odd apparition in the diminishing light—and a groan came from his chest, a wheezing, a cough.

"Hello George," Margery said.

Her voice was calming, resigned, maybe because she knew she would have to postpone those dry clothes, but she'd at least spoken to him—his name and not mine.

I studied George while he talked aimlessly about the flora and fauna and forest rodents. Despite his good nature, he didn't look healthy— aside from his decidedly awkward frame that he'd obviously been born with, his head was slightly misshapen on one side near the back, almost imperceptible because he boasted that incongruously long, relatively thick hair. But, if anything, I have an odd penchant for noticing details about people's physicality—I suppress my observations because I am often overcome by a largely imagined plight of those others and soon I am afflicted with the misery of all humankind. Certainly that is hyperbole, but you get the idea. Was the bulge on George's head the result of a fall— maybe a bungee jump? Or something more sinister?

George was affable enough, comfortable in his own thin skin. He made me wonder how I, who by all appearances looked healthier by a wide margin, could be beset by aches and pains and anxieties about never again being able to hike into the wilderness and discover such a surprising place, where the people seemed somewhat crazy, but on the whole satisfied with themselves and their lives.

George described his excitement about finding what he called a "cantharellus cibarius" at this altitude, and he went on to describe mushrooms from various parts of the world, some with the power to restore sex drive, and I pretended to listen to his full account of his day

Margery

in the woods, nodding and agreeing it was all fascinating. "Well," George said abruptly, "I'm off …" But he went nowhere, chatting awhile longer, speaking only to Margery about the wind and weather patterns and what a nice day it was, then finally saying goodbye, hugging and smiling and patting her on the back as though headed to another planet. I think he said something to her about me, but missed it—was the ringing in my ears returning? I'd read that it could be from hearing loss.

With George gone, Margery took a deep breath, and I sensed she was allowing distance between them before heading back. Long shadows were creeping up the eastern ridge, visible through the trees, a bright glow on the treetops—the sun slipping away from us all—along with my opportunity to learn more about her.

"Guess I'd better pitch my tent." But I wasn't sure what telling her that might have accomplished. Would she offer to help, when setting up my one-person tent required such little effort? So I hastily added, "What do you call this place?"

"Most of us refer to it as the 'town.'" Margery looked at me. "Sometimes I call it 'eternity.'"

I didn't know how to respond, except to note the quiet, almost serene nature of her voice, while I unrolled my tent, inserted the poles, and listened to my stomach rumbling so loudly I could hear it over the crashing of the water.

Margery had already started off, but she stopped. "Are you hungry?"

That was much easier to answer. "Yes, starving."

"Join me then."

"Would love to … will my stuff be okay here?"

"Of course. No one here wants 'stuff.'"

That might have been so, but I felt uneasy leaving my tent and backpack unattended—it was my home, my pack having been lugged into the mountains, by me, for most of my lifetime, worn and ripped and repaired but still functional, with added compartments, and a solid frame. I dug out a long-sleeved shirt, cinched down all the straps, and put the shirt on while walking quietly behind Margery in the retreating light, comfortable in her presence, wondering where she lived, where she cooked meals and breathed the air of this paradise—who was she? Her home was nearest the forest and stream and her cliff, a combination log cabin and green sided home—the sort of place you'd expect a billionaire investor to show off as his third vacation home, but as you looked closer it lacked the showy ostentation you might expect—gilded kitchen faucets, stylish cabinetry, wall-to-ceiling mirrors—none of that. Just pragmatism and disrepair.

While Margery went down the hall to change, I stood in the kitchen—light and airy, green-blue peeling paint, and small cracks needing patchwork near the dirty beige refrigerator that clunked occasionally. She returned wearing a dress that reminded me of hippies and Woodstock and flower power and *all we are saying is give peace a chance.* She opened the refrigerator and pulled out vegetable snacks, salad, fruits, grains; all the foods that screamed health.

To say Margery and I had a conversation while cooking wouldn't be accurate—I chopped vegetables and measured things according to her instructions as we exchanged words needed for the task at hand, but not much beyond that—as if moving beyond the preparation for the meal required a commitment neither of us could make—perhaps knowing that once we passed that barrier, we would rush to some sort of culmination or climax, and such a ride required thought before climbing on—and there was an enormous amount of food for just the two of us, so I made a joke.

"Do we have enough?"

She looked at me and hesitated, then allowed herself the interaction. "You look like you need to bulk up ... but we're having guests."

Kaylee arrived, followed by a pair I'd met in passing earlier, although I couldn't remember their names. As we sat at Margery's table under a faux western chandelier, they were introduced as Henry and Jackie, a fine-looking couple that reminded me of my parents in a retirement community, where they'd long forgotten who they were but had left a trail of pictures, mementos, jewelry, and furniture auctioned off, and who I had expected to die years ago.

All our names struck me as funny—Henry, Jackie, Kaylee, Margery, and me, Jeremy, as if we were a hockey team with forced nicknames. Given my struggle with names in general, even my own, I thought it was hilarious, and I laughed loudly—no doubt obnoxiously.

Margery

Margery smiled. "Yes," she said, smoothly, "somehow we all end in a rising, rhythmic, silly vowel sound."

For a moment, I tried to guess her career—a teacher?—then let it go, not wanting to know anything beyond the pleasure of her company.

Henry and Jackie exuded good humor tinged with anxiety—something I'd struggled with—mostly coming from Henry, but from Jackie as well, especially when she looked at him. They seemed okay otherwise, trying hard to stay cheerful, as they complimented me and Margery for the delicious meal, and I joked about having little to no talent in food preparation.

The conversation skipped along the surface, shifting politely from food and hiking to the weather and home maintenance—things that quickly fade into insignificance. I suppressed my curiosity about this place, where I'd somehow ended up without intention. Did I really want to know? Not really, preferring the satisfying taste of cucumber and red onion and squash and brown rice stirred in with balsamic marinade, and listening to Margery talk about a cool breeze she'd felt early this morning coming off the stream.

I was nodding at Henry, acknowledging and approving of his using duct tape to extend the life of notebook binders, while his wife Jackie struggled to appear engaged, eating little, and becoming increasingly agitated, shifting in her seat, eyes darting from one person to the next, then suddenly blurting out a story about her childhood irrelevant to the conversation. Henry squeezed her arm and stared at her kindly but firmly as if saying, *nobody cares about that dear*, and she settled down, stirring her food with her fork but not eating.

Kaylee fidgeted and kept glancing over her shoulder, ears attuned, and I couldn't help but ask, "So where's Josh?" She stared at me—my previous excitement at her youth having receded, thankfully; having reasoned my way through it. Our baser instincts and thoughts don't need to always come to fruition, do they? Or had my yearning merely been replaced?

Margery passed the potatoes, literally—and figuratively, in that she was diverting thoughts away from my apparently insensitive question—seasoned sliced potatoes, and I gladly accepted, my inquiry about Josh ignored and apparently forgotten. Kaylee and Josh, as I had suspected, must have had an argument, and it was for now a subject best avoided.

Henry and Jackie cleared the table, helped with the dishes, chatted as amiably as any dinner guests might, and then excused themselves, and only with their departure did I feel the lightness that comes from carrying a heavy backpack all day and removing it at camp—the heaviness from Henry and Jackie was so intangible that I didn't know it was weighing me down until it was gone.

"What's wrong with them?" I asked.

Again, I'd asked an inappropriate question and immediately, for the millionth time, became conscious of my desire for solitude in the wilderness. Kaylee and Margery ignored me while finishing the meal clean-up, and then they headed for the front door. I followed but lingered, hoping Kaylee would leave first as she opened the door, the cool night air filling the room, further stirring my desire to seek warmth from Margery as we all stepped onto the front porch, a muted glow from the stars and the waning moon lighting the road. Kaylee stumbled and fell into my arms, and she held on tightly squeezing me while my arms lay lightly on her shoulders. She held me too long—how was I supposed to react, should I reciprocate? I felt like a Josh replacement. She hugged longer than I could understand, and released me to the cool night.

While watching Kaylee disappear into the darkness, wondering again what had happened to Josh, Margery touched my shoulder, a gentle push as if to guide me. Or just pushing me away? All I wanted was hold to her the way Kaylee had held me, and I fought to rationalize—maybe my feelings were merely the weariness of a traveler who longs for rest; maybe someone, who in reality, wanted to return to the life he had before hiking into this forest. I didn't move, standing at the top of the steps, waiting for more. Her measured response revealed only the slightest impatience.

"Do you need help finding your way?"

Help, I thought, and felt ill-prepared for the sudden torrent of confusing emotions, and I tried to defend myself from myself, ultimately failing of course—*no I don't want to go back to camp, I want to touch every part of you, I want to enjoy our flesh together while we still can, to resist the inevitable slow but steady progression of nature, I want to embrace eternity, locked in each other's arms, immortalized as constellations or entombed in volcanic ash or reincarnated as one person, together flinging ourselves through the universe*—such were my wildly romantic thoughts, flushing me with emotion I had thought dead forever, but now resurrected in this strange remote town in this bucolic setting. I felt so close to that instant of perfection, fleeting as it may be, if only I could lie in the arms of Margery.

I usually calculated my moves. But not this time, this time I felt my movements uncontrollable, surging over me, impossible to stop. I leaned forward to kiss her.

"I can't," she said, pushing me away.

I stared, stunned, but recovered quickly enough—my protective shield had been cultivated over a lifetime of disappointments, failures, and tragedy. And now it reliably rose back into place, working properly, working as well as it ever had, sliding over my body, flattening my countenance, and allowing my polite reply. "I understand."

Of course, I understood nothing.

I thought of Kaylee and Josh—they loved each other, enough to become disappointed and angry at each other.

Margery touched me again, cruelly I thought, and gave me a gentle squeeze and a nudge into the dark.

4

THE TOWN HAD VERY FEW LIGHTS and the gravel and dirt roads were lit only by the starlight, the moon having slipped beyond the cliff, its glow hidden, and my camp somewhere in the dark woods next to the stream. Disoriented, I walked from the end of the road, gliding onto the trail straight toward the now black and looming cliff and searched the woods for any hint of the trail, and heard rustling in the bushes—maybe some wildlife. Deer? Moose? Bear? Hesitant to go further, I pressed on, following a narrow footpath, hopefully the one Margery and I had taken earlier, maybe the one trampled down by her treks from the stream, and I imagined the bungee cord still dangling from the cliff where there was an overhang, the only spot that would not smash her to a pulpy mess. She would have to leap out far enough to miss the protruding rock and hope the cord did not snap or rub raw on the sharp cliff edge, swinging back into the hollowed-out portion—a precision jump to say the least. It must've taken some practice. How did she do it the first time?

Someone stumbled from the brush and fell onto the footpath in front of me, wheezing and coughing. I knelt to help whoever it was, and felt sure it was George when grabbing his thick arm and helping him to

Margery

his feet, the two of us outlined in the dark, his slightly misshapen head silhouetted against the glimmer of the stream, and asked if he was okay.

"Not as steady as I once was," he said.

I was going to ask what he was doing wandering through the forest at night, but he asked me first, and I gave him my perfectly sensible answer—going to camp—to which he replied, "So you like being alone in the dark?"

Did I? I'd certainly spent many nights camping by myself, in the dark, alone—even when sleeping with someone else, weren't we alone? Unless we were connected during those moments of merging together as one. Why did we long so much for that? Merely to create children who became stressed out adults, themselves struggling to survive. I was thinking too much, and admittedly, they weren't cheerful thoughts.

"Didn't mean," George said, "to make you uncomfortable."

"Oh no, not at all … just made me think, that's all."

"Oh, I apologize for that. Too much reflection. Be careful of that. Sometimes it brings on too much reality. That can make you cynical. Be happy, man! Change your thoughts and you can change your life. Choose to be happy. The pessimist may be right, but the optimist has more fun." Then he said basically this—Cough. Cough. Wheeze. Inhale. Wheeze.

I asked again if he was okay.

"I'm okay if you're okay." Cough.

Was I okay? Somehow, despite his exhortations to be positive, George was bringing me down. I was just beginning to feel more optimistic about Margery, reinterpreting her touch on my shoulder and her gentle squeeze on my arm, but after listening to him, all I could think about was her puzzling words: "I can't." How was I supposed to create another reality from those words? *You can*, I thought.

"Yes," I said. "Yes you *can*."

"That's the spirit," George said. "Now you get it!"

I didn't get anything really, but was glad he thought so—he wrapped his bulky arms around me and squeezed tight.

"I love you man," he said, making me feel obligated to respond with equal affection.

"Yeah," I said.

I held his shoulders and squeezed, feigning warmth while pushing him away. We stared at each other, George smiling, his teeth so big and boisterous they seemed to shine in the night, and now, facing him, something about the darkness made it easier to see the huge orange-sized lump swelling behind his right ear, pushing beyond his thick hair—how did I not see the extent of it before? George patted my arm and turned away, a cough receding in the distance. I stood. Alone. In the dark.

Even so, I found my way home to my tent, and slept soundly, exhausted beyond my mind's capacity to keep my body tense, and upon waking could barely move, the stiffness and tightness more than what I'd come to expect.

I lay there watching the cliff blaze alive with morning sunlight and the dew dropping from leaves, dropping on my sagging tent. And I rose, half-expecting someone to arrive with a pleasant greeting—but no one came—and I made myself a cup of coffee, the whir of my camp stove reassuring in the morning light, sipping my coffee and facing the chore of packing up—I almost never stayed in the same campsite more than a night—two at most—on rare occasion, more. Was this one of those occasions?

The hot coffee was good, but it aroused a dull ache in my jaw—a cracked tooth ignored for too long. I shuffled the pain aside, knowing that escaping into the wilderness alone helped cure almost all of my ailments in the past—the tooth only served as a reminder of what I must do later when facing the onslaught of daily life back from where I'd escaped.

In a fantasy world, I could choose to never go back—chuck it all and stay forever, wandering through this forest. *Always an option*, I thought, knowing that I had never taken that option before and was never going to.

Leaving my camp feeling well-rested and confident, I headed toward town, hoping to see Margery. I was smitten. I knew it and was prepared to work my way through it—my thoughts degenerating into George-like phrases. *Now you get it, man!*

I didn't know why I felt so attracted to Margery, nor did I want to know, because the more I knew about her, surely the feeling I had now would subside and dissipate—of course the attraction could never last—

normal for it to settle into respect and a more nuanced affection. But it could also descend into a rut—routine boredom and neglect. I had experienced both. I wanted to enjoy forever my fleeting feeling of being so alive and energetic and purposeful. So, it was with a competing desire to run into Margery's arms, and to move slowly and cautiously, that I walked a tightrope of feelings at once exhilarating and dangerous. When we slept together, I'd want it to last, I'd want us to come to the edge of desire and withdraw and go back again, reveling in each other's primal essence.

It was this mind and body fullness and anticipatory flush that was shocked to grotesque reality when I found George lying in the brush on his back, staring up at the trees or beyond to the dawning pale blue sky, his arm crooked and hand cupped close to his mouth as if to whisper one last optimistic entreaty—smile—and yes, he was smiling, mouth set for perpetual happiness, teeth straight and white and no longer needed, his head tilted slightly to the left. I knelt over him, and tried to rouse him, yelling, "George! George!" But to no avail. I tried to push his arm away from his face, but it was too stiff and his skin was cold. I sat in the path and frowned while looking toward the town, but saw nothing.

I could have helped George get into a bed, and made him warm for the night so that whatever was ailing him could have been cared for, but I'd been anxious to get away from his overbearing conviviality and unrelenting good mood—I'd felt uncomfortable with it. Was it because he was too gregarious or was it a flaw in my much-too-introspective character?

If I had accepted him unconditionally and listened to him, maybe I could have helped him. But I'll tell you why I didn't, so I might assuage my guilt—in the end, there was nothing I could have done. I should have tried anyway—but I had already spent endless years trying to help others less fortunate, while I struggled to maintain the middle-class dream, only to have the dream collapse, pushing me toward the sort of insanity I was always trying to pull others away from.

I think, with George, I was just worn out. No excuse, really. He wasn't anyone special to me, at best a new acquaintance. But I should have helped him. I sat there staring at his lifeless, eerily happy face and cried. It was as if, in George, I had failed in my own life; optimistic or not, happy or not, okay or not, I had failed to make even a minimal effort, at the very least to hold him while he died. George died alone in the dark.

I looked around, waiting, thinking—*Someone save me from this.*

Wiping away my tears, I rose to my feet, standing there, looking at him, and then heard, "Oh, hello, you're still here?"

It was Margery, and for an instant I wished she had arrived thirty seconds sooner to catch me weeping, so that for once I might be on the receiving end of empathy—and felt childish.

"He's dead," I said.

Margery stood next to me. "Yes," she said. "I see …"

That was it? Why didn't she break down? Certainly she'd known the man, at least longer than I had. Was she incapable of the feeling I wanted from her?

"I'm going to jump," she said.

"What about him?" I was captivated by her nonchalance, or peacefulness—her demeanor saying what I was thinking—*George isn't going anywhere, is he?*—and I wanted to go with her. "What if someone else finds him?"

But Margery was already on her way, resolute, hiking upstream, and I hastily broke branches and covered George in the brush to hide him from some unsuspecting soul who might be shocked at his passing—it was the least I could do for the living.

I caught up to Margery when she paused at my camp, assessing my home, the way I'd arranged my backpack, stashed my gear. She glanced at me, then turned and climbed onto a boulder, making her way across the stream, leaping over a spout of water surging white downstream. On the other side, I followed her, hiking over a thick bed of pine needles, tall pine growing straight to the sky out of a steep incline—a barely discernible path—probably created by Margery's footsteps, or shared with wildlife. She emerged onto a talus slope, jagged rocks sliding into my ankles with each step, then onto clean rock where we started a harrowing scramble up deep fissures and cracks, often having to use handholds on exposed faces—not, strictly speaking, technical rock climbing, requiring ropes and protection, but close, close enough for me to wonder how I would get down, because I'd been around long enough to know that getting down safely was more difficult than going up—what the hell was I doing? But in mid-scramble, I felt Margery's magnetism pulling me, growing ever more powerful in this dangerous ascent with few choices for coming down other than following her, or falling, a long, frightening fall that could kill me. Even as I climbed, my mind tended to overanalyze. What was going on here? I tried to find some use in melodrama, muttering, "Oh, Margery, why have you done this to me, why am I such a fool?" It was a feeble attempt to make sense of things. Then, trying reason, I concluded that if I'd stayed around the town long enough I would have eventually hiked to the top of the cliff on my own because I'm always hiking further into the wilderness, always pushing the edge, wanting the summit.

Margery made two unnerving moves, hand jambs along a crack, before hoisting herself onto the crown of the rock. I followed, exposed in the wind, moving quickly before I had too much time to think, and joined her standing in the trees just beneath the top of the cliff.

"Impressive," she said.

I bragged. "I've done some climbing."

She glanced at me, and I hoped she was referring to my climbing and not the view.

In my younger years, this experience would have been thrilling, but now, while still exciting and satisfying, it was tempered with too much pragmatism. How would I get down? Down there, where George's rigid hand was cupped to his grin, whispering some unspeakable happiness. I'd seen death before, but George was different. So was Margery, and so was Kaylee, and the others.

Margery veered into the trees onto another narrow, steep path, and soon we were standing near the cliff's edge, scrub pine behind us tapering into forest, and we were overlooking the town, the tops of trees moving like a symphony with the wind and the far ridge washed out and bright in the sun, the town so small now that it blended into the forest and, unless you were looking, disappeared altogether. In the distance to the south, beyond the gorge, the long valley twisting down to serpentine roads and beyond—the civilization I was continually dependent upon and continually escaping.

Margery crouched at the edge, grabbed her bungee cord, then stood and started hauling it up hand over hand, curling it at her feet. The cord was anchored into the rock with strands of blue webbing and one long strand reaching to a tree.

Why was I here, with her, on this edge? Did she want me to watch? Join her? Jump after her? But she hadn't actually invited me—I had decided on my own to follow her.

She sat, methodically attaching the cord to her ankle and her waist. I knew nothing about bungee cord jumping, but it seemed to me that there should have been a safety rope. I was waiting for an explanation, but she was ignoring me.

"Is there an easier way down?" I asked.

She looked at me, and her expression appeared to match mine, both of us wondering why I had followed her.

"I don't know," she said.

"So," I said, "you climb down the same route?"

"No. I jump."

The implication hit me hard—*she couldn't have just climbed up here and jumped.* Without knowing. Without climbing up and down a few times to study the viability of such an activity.

I stared at her standing on the edge in the midmorning brightness, her arms sinewy and her face weathered and, at least for that moment, she radiated the hope of a bright future, an optimist like George, although much softer in her expression of that future—her intelligence, strength, and beauty, at least to my besotted eyes, and I had to admit, she might have been slightly crazy. Maybe some types of "crazy" come with an intensity we are all drawn to.

Margery glanced at me while she quickly adjusted her anchor webbing, moving it about ten feet, and my curiosity drove me to the edge with her, and I peered over; the jump—or fall—from this reality, looked much more dangerous than I'd originally thought—adjusting her "departure" point placed her leap right above a massive rock, requiring a running leap to clear—otherwise she'd bounce—I imagined all sorts of grisly scenarios—her limbs snapping, Margery tumbling like a rag doll, leg ripped off, unconscious or dead body dangling just above the clear stream.

"No way I'm doing that."

She chuckled, a quiet soothing laugh, as if we'd shared a funny moment in a city park watching the bustle of life irrelevant to our affection for one another. "Nobody asked you."

"Yes, but ..."

Margery

"It's okay," she said. "You don't have to jump."

"Neither do you."

Her brow furrowed, puzzled; sincerely I think. And, as I thought about it, I was also puzzled. One of the very things that drew me to her, that nearly overwhelmed me, at least in the abstract, was her daring, her sense of adventure—but did she really have to jump?

"Yes," she said, "I do." She turned and ran, leaping, hurling herself into mid-air, screaming and yelling with joy, hanging in the air, lighter than the gravity that pulled her down.

Panic rose in my chest, nearly squeezing my heart to a stop, and I thought I'd missed my chance, and how stupid, even at my age, that I should hesitate in telling someone how I felt about them—always trying to define the feeling before expressing it.

Even now I question it.

I inched my way to the edge, the bungee cord pulsing like a heartbeat, searching the rocks for blood—couldn't be sure—rock patterns are deceiving and surely that dark spot was not Margery but merely a shadow, a crack, a patch of moss.

Leaning into the air, flirting with disaster, I called for her, "Margery!"

Was that her? An echo? I moved very carefully along the edge searching for a better angle, but could only see far into the distance, the valley and the twisting roads. I pulled on the bungee cord and it felt like a humming telephone cable, taut, alive with a slight slowing vibration, presumably still attached to her, telling me that she was still there and alive. But shouldn't it have gone slack when she released herself into the water? Was her unconscious body dangling on the other end?

5

I WAITED FOR THE CORD TO SLACKEN, waited as long as I could stand it—time interminably slow, my patience wearing thin. I tugged on the cord again—still taut—and backed away from the precipice. I searched for the route down, couldn't find it, and started my descent anyway, soon faced with a ledge, the next step a fall into the treetops. I moved along the ledge, and found a steep narrow gully of loose rocks crumbling and sliding around my ankles with each lunging stride, a haphazard, barely controlled descent, hands breaking my slide, shredding my skin—leveling into the forest, coming to another steep drop-off, having to retrace my steps, picking my way along the sloping terrain, slowly, stopping often to gain my bearings, glancing back to the cliff and peeking through branches, searching for a glimpse of the town.

It took me a lot longer than it should have, often losing my way, but finally reaching a stable slope, hiking down through forest to the boulders where we had begun our ascent only a couple hours ago … but seeming much longer. I crossed the white water, climbed down near my camp, and moved quickly to the clearing, where I saw her cord

Margery

dangling from the cliff, expecting to see her leg ripped from her torso. But there was nothing. Where was Margery?

The stream cut into the cliff, providing only enough space for her to avoid smashing into jagged rock and deep enough for her to touch the smooth stones on the bottom. Her jumps defied survival. Why would she continually risk certain death or worse, and where was she now? I scanned the surrounding forest. Why couldn't she wait for me, reassure me? I thought about going to her house, looking for her there, and felt a sudden revulsion at passing George's body, hidden by me, hoping to help the others, keep them from the distress of tripping over a dead body, but now I wished I'd dragged the body into the middle of the wide trail near town and someone else had taken responsibility for it.

I retreated to my camp—my tent, my backpack leaning against the rock just as I'd left it—and felt a sudden urge to move on. I rolled up the tent and stuffed it into my pack. I filled my water bottle, dropped in an iodine tablet, cinched down the pack straps, and then heaved it onto my back like an old friend. I needed to get away from this place, doing what I had always done; run away from my feelings, run away from the complexities of the heart because I was terrible at it, especially when I became too involved, too invested in the people around me.

My hand bled and my legs were scraped and I thought—*must have had a good time*—but now it was time to leave. My plan was to hike back through town and retrace the route Kaylee and Josh had taken me on. Might be a little difficult because I hadn't paid attention to how I'd gotten here—what trail might take me back to where I'd come from? I might have to ask someone, anyone who might know.

With my heavy pack snug, part of my body again, I hiked along the stream toward the clearing and the path to town, trying to avert my eyes while skipping past George's stiff arm, his hand reaching out of the brush I'd covered him with. I grimaced, trying not to look, not wanting to see his happy death, wanting to bury it all into my ever-accumulating past.

Afternoon clouds were billowing up over the town, turning from white cumulus to a slowly moving dark line promising a downpour. I hiked up the central road, past Margery's house, saw no one, and continued on, determined despite the ominous weather. Then a sudden gust swirled out of the sky like the hand of God, pushing me back and lashing at me with bursts of horizontal rain.

"Jeremy."

Kaylee waved me toward her, and I followed onto her front porch as the wind whirled and swept in on us. She pulled me through her front door, into a narrow foyer, where I slid out of my backpack. I was dripping, soaked, and Kaylee as well.

"We were looking for you," she said.

"We?"

"Margery ..."

I shook my head like a wet dog, dripping onto old hardwood floor, the rain pounding against the small blue house in waves, gusts one after the other, pounding against the front windows. *Margery hadn't been looking for me*, I thought. *She could have easily found me if she'd wanted.* "So she's okay?" I said.

Kaylee touched my shoulder and it looked like her left eye was drifting apart from her face, and she squinted, forcing the errant eye into focus, or submission, realigning her sight directly upon me. "Yes," she said with sudden enthusiasm. "Yes!" As if her voice had been taken over by the crazy eye.

Then she lunged toward me and I instinctively put up my hands to fend her off and accidentally hit her in the nose, even though she wasn't at all threatening and my response reflected my own troubles, my own wary nature, always ready to defend against the next onslaught. She leaned past my resistance and threw her arms around my neck and held me as if we were long lost lovers.

I held on loosely—not sure what to do—recalling my initial reaction to her—the older man trying to reclaim his youth—and felt Kaylee was more than ever like my daughter, who was probably older than Kaylee and who I'd left long ago, parting with her and my son and my wife, as I went traveling from one disappearing forest to another, exploring, trying to regain my youth by outrunning my age, and by outrunning something else troubling me, scientific realities about my health that I couldn't accept and had buried so deep into my subconscious I'd forgotten them entirely and worked hard to keep forgotten during my long slogs through the disappearing wilderness. Now with Kaylee still holding onto me, holding on forever, I recalled the day I'd started on this particular journey and my brief conversation with my daughter over airwaves breaking up, the batteries of our conversation on the edge of dying, lasting only long enough for us to say hello and goodbye again as we'd become accustomed to over many years, and I could not now remember if I told her I loved her.

And perhaps it was recollection of that conversation that separated Kaylee from my daughter, and made Kaylee someone so similar yet entirely different that I could feel myself relax in her embrace, and she kissed my cheek, and receded from my arms, taking my hand, squeezing hard. "Yes?" she said, and I noticed her eye drooping, falling instead of rising. She smiled, and it made her face look odd, almost disfigured, but also, in her gaze, lots of affection and some kind of love and therefore beauty.

"Yes," I answered, or at least thought so, puzzled by her "Yes" in the form of a question.

The storm had receded and, as if by magic, I heard Margery calling from outside, her voice replacing the wind. I hastily released Kaylee's hand and distanced myself from her, feeling guilty for even the possibility of creating a false impression.

"We'd better go," I said. "Let her know I've been found."

"Yes," Kaylee said, and I began to wonder about her vocabulary, her attentiveness to her surroundings, so unlike when I'd first met her with Josh, the thought of him now making his absence even more curious.

Kaylee shuddered, shut her eyes tight and suddenly returned to this world, as if she'd fought off the grim reaper himself. When, in reality—or at least in my reality—in that moment, she was merely fighting an innocent desire, for me it appeared—and I'd long since learned that there was nothing to brag about when it came to fickle desire. On the other hand, I was surprised at how all-encompassing and good it felt to be wanted by another human being, regardless of its nature.

We went outside where the rain still dripped from the trees and the smell of cleansing water matched the gentle roar in the distance, in the hills and mountains, a thousand or so rivulets and waterfalls cascading down and reverberating in the basin.

Margery looked at me, as though, I thought, I was Josh. "Come on you two," she said. "We've got to take care of George."

I had for the most part successfully forgotten about George. Now I had to reverse that process to help "take care" of him. Hopefully, I'd do a better job of it.

With my emotions vacillating between desire and fear, I distanced myself from Kaylee and walked with Margery, trying to puzzle my way through her resistance, her "I can't," wondering what that meant exactly. She couldn't. But if she could, would she want to embrace me as Kaylee had? Was it possible that she wanted me as I did her? Clearly, there was something that blocked her ability to express it, but I chose to believe that she had strong feelings for me.

Soon we were joined by the group of hikers, and then the dinner couple, Henry and his wife Jackie, who looked confused by the gathering of maybe the entire town, with a few exceptions—no teenager, no old woman in bright shoes, and no Josh—had they just disappeared, some sort of rapture? Several carried shovels and someone handed me one—why me and not the heavy guy in the sweat pants?—and I suppose I felt honored in some bizarre way.

Someone had already removed the brush from George, and we stood in ragged semi-circle, staring at his peculiarly stiffened body. Not only was I was feeling guilty about leaving him there, but also about my surprise that so many came to watch him being buried. Why would I think that nobody cared about George? I leaned on my shovel, expecting some sort of service, or ritual, a few words at least, some mumbo jumbo, holy Allahs, praise the Lords, something, anything, but someone started digging, and those of us with shovels followed along, whacking away at branches, prying out big rocks—digging a grave right where he died.

While digging, helping roll away a rock, and standing back to give someone else a turn, I again wondered about Josh and listened to the generally matter-of-fact and occasionally lighthearted conversation, just as likely to be about the passing storm as it was about George—from what I could glean from the talk, George loved to gather berries and mushrooms and watercress and other leafy edibles—his salads apparently were "to die for" and I smiled not so much at the word choice, but that nobody made a joke about it. Maybe I was just being

Margery

smug, or maybe nobody else cared about such trivial puns at that moment. George's salads, someone said, were so healthy that they would allow him to gather mushrooms and watercress for eternity.

"If you want to," Kaylee said, "you can say that George is part of everything."

"Yes," the dinner guest Henry said, "he's in our salad."

Apparently, at least he had a sense of humor, and made me wish I'd made my death joke, and through telling it, gained some acceptance and softened Margery. We renewed our effort to get the job done and after a few feet hit solid rock.

Henry said, "He won't mind being on the rocks."

Margery and I and a couple hikers rolled George's body into the shallow grave, his face in the dirt, his stiff arm keeping him from settling in comfortably, so we pushed and tugged, and adjusted, and arranged, but couldn't find a way to make him fit. He was more or less on his back, but his arm was sticking out too much. If we wanted to cover him completely, we would have to spend hours dislodging rocks, digging the grave in a different direction or finding a new site. Margery was standing closest to him and she looked at Henry, who nodded, and she studied the others, apparently making sure no one objected, then she stomped on George's arm, snapping it, the sound like a branch breaking in a storm. She pushed the arm across his chest, elbow down but hand still cupped against his chin, so that now he looked as if he were in the traditional "thinker" pose.

We stood for a moment, and again I expected some holy words, but nothing came and we almost simultaneously started shoveling the dirt back onto his body, and we gathered big rocks from along the stream and piled them onto George's shallow grave—the evening descending upon us.

I was hungry again—if out on a day hike with friends I might say "starving to death" but refrained, still not sure anyone would think it funny, assuring myself that I had matured enough to know when hyperbole might not be appropriate.

People were wandering away in pairs and groups, someone graciously taking my shovel while I lingered behind, staying close to Margery, waiting for her to invite me to dinner again, the evening light accentuating her strong cheekbones, yet soft eyes, and her slight, close-lipped smile remained alluring yet puzzling, hiding some joke that I'd yet to be privy to.

"I would," I said formally, "invite you to dine with me tonight, to reciprocate, but all I have is gorp."

Margery looked at Kaylee. "We're eating with Henry and his wife tonight."

"We?" I asked.

"You can come as my guest."

"I'd like that."

So I'd gone from wanting to leave town to accepting a dinner invitation—gone from being annoyed at Margery to being hopeful as we hiked again up the road to her house where she went in to wash off, and I had to go with Kaylee because my backpack was there—Kaylee changing into a sundress and a wool sweater top. I stared at my dirty pack and decided to go as is, zipping up my coat against the cool evening.

6

HENRY AS THE PRACTICAL HUSBAND and Jackie his nervous wife lived in a ranch house on the east end of town near the ridge, a short walk, as all the homes were a short walk away. The town felt smaller than it had a few days ago—a matter of perspective—coming from many days in the woods to a group of houses made the town appear larger.

Inside, the hallways and rooms were cluttered with artifacts from their long and rich lives, paintings that looked to be originals although I couldn't name the artists, landscapes of mountains and forests and one of Henry sitting, back straight on horseback holding the reins, posing, and in uniform, but as I looked closer, it appeared to be very early twentieth century, pre-World War I, so it clearly couldn't have been him—maybe his father or grandfather. There were, oddly, no photographs, no pictures of them when they were young, no photos of smiling grandchildren, nothing to indicate that any of the artifacts belonged to them at all. The large kitchen had white stark walls, recently painted, incongruent with the rest of the house, as if this room specifically needed to be sterile. Henry's wife Jackie, while still exuding an underlying nervousness, was pleasant enough, and in the bright light

Margery

of their kitchen, she looked very old. We had a few drinks at the counter and chatted as if we were suburban neighbors. I looked at Henry and he also seemed old, and I considered asking if that was him in the painting.

We went to the dining room—Kaylee, Margery, and I sat on one side of the long rectangular table, Henry at one end, and Jackie at the other—and we were joined by several people whom I'd met as part of the hiker group.

The conversation started innocently enough when someone mentioned the weather but from there quickly devolved into passionate and widely divergent political and religious expressions, highly informed and surprisingly respectful but ultimately depressing—silence falling like volcanic ash—everyone chewing their food while staring vacantly—probably trying to rid themselves, as I was, of the all too familiar images of starving and dying children.

Someone asked Jackie if she and Henry had gone to the meadow today and Jackie suddenly lost her anxiety and told what she clearly thought was a wildly humorous story about Henry falling in a creek while trying to take her picture, but it wasn't in this meadow—it was a meadow far removed in distance and time, a meadow and a mountain stream in a foreign land where they were young and happy and forever alive, and she now laughed heartily and long and happily until it subsided and the others all nodded and smiled knowingly—they'd heard this story before—as perhaps all old friends acknowledge stories repeatedly told and shared as a gift to each other, except that this group displayed a weariness at the telling, as if it were a story told too often, its joyous effects diminishing with each nearly identical rendition.

The conversation easily shifted to individual adventures, hiking and climbing around the town, then to me asking practical questions about energy sources—solar mostly—and supplies—their fresh fruits and vegetables—no roads out of the basin that I could see and no cars or trucks. Henry mostly answered my questions, but a few of the others added detail—there was one precarious road snaking along the edge of the gorge, treacherous in good conditions, impassable in bad, and two old trucks parked near the southwest corner—there used to be three trucks, but one slipped a tire over the edge and hung there for days blocking the road before they had to push it off—not many people come here—about twenty people at the moment. Someone made a passing reference to Margery's jump, asking how it went today, which she said was good. I gulped some of the delicious red wine that Henry kept pouring everyone.

"So, Margery," I asked, "I've been dying to ask you …" The others burst into laughter and I felt an unusual twinge of embarrassment at my timing, an unintentional joke more suited to George's happy burial. I pressed on. "Are you a professional … I don't know, adventurer, bungee cord jumper? Is there such a thing?"

Margery smiled. "Not really, no."

I stared at her, and she met my gaze full on, not backing down, as if to say *No I'm not crazy*. I waited for her to say something more, to offer a reasonable explanation, but she quickly shifted the conversation toward Kaylee, telling her how much she liked her sundress and something about how refreshing today's storm was.

No one mentioned George directly. But I was fighting images of him coming back to life and imploring me to be happy, and was waiting for someone to express sadness in his passing, or at least acknowledge that the man had existed. Would it have been impolite to ask about him? Then I wondered about medical care. Clearly, George had been ill. Was there anyone to take care of him, to diagnose him? My tongue wandered to my molar; what felt like a new crack, a sharp edge that I hadn't noticed before. Did they have doctors and dentists?

"I know," I said, "everyone seems healthy …" Again, there was some general amusement at my comment. "But you must have a doctor, right?"

Henry looked at me. "I'm a doctor."

I exhaled and responded enthusiastically, "Great."

"What seems to be the trouble?"

I felt odd consulting him while everyone was looking at me. "Nothing really …"

"It's okay," he said. "We're not particularly formal."

"Well, my tooth …" I instinctively felt it with my tongue.

Henry shook his head, the others shifted in their seats, struggling to keep quiet. "George was the dentist."

Then the table itself rumbled with laughter—including Margery—the first I'd seen her express such unbridled good cheer, and it made me happy, able to share some strange pleasure with her. As the mirth was settling, Jackie suddenly began telling her story about Henry falling into the creek, telling it more or less exactly as she had before, as if she had never before told the story.

The meal, as it had been at Margery's the previous night, was fresh and healthy with organic vigor—vegetables, fruit, a hint of a familiar "spice" that became prominent with dessert, a plate of cookies loaded with cannabis. By the time Margery and I, and Kaylee, made it outside into the starlit night with the moon glowing beyond the cliff, we were, or at least I was, as high as the moon and the stars like a big pizza pie and I walked on top of the darkness, floating, yet also stumbling on unforeseeable bumps—I wanted to touch Margery, as we walked, with Kaylee on one side and Margery on the other—and it seemed like Kaylee was hanging around Margery all the time—why was she here now?

"Wow," I said to nobody in particular.

"Yes," Margery responded warmly.

"Where are we going?"

"Nowhere in particular."

But we were headed toward Kaylee's home, and Margery's beyond, in the shadow of the dark cliff and we slowed our pace, and I stopped, and stared up into the universe and sensed it lifting me into space where we would be eternally happy.

Kaylee turned toward me and slid into my arms as she had done before but this time every part of my body sang alive with something other than desire—with something, I hesitate to say, spiritual, and I looked for Margery. She was slowly moving away in the dark, floating into outer space, and I cried *Wait up, Margery!* my voice struggling to find her, and I took Kaylee's hand as we drifted through the night into Margery's orbit and although I couldn't see her fully in the starlight, she seemed sad—or something in my own past was just now emerging. She took my other hand and like tethered spacecraft, we formed a circle beneath the universe, the three of us looking up at the stars and slowly rotating, three linked bodies, brought together in space by our gravitational pull on each other.

Then it became a little awkward, as such movements on earth can, and I released their hands, Kaylee reluctant to let go, and I felt self-conscious, wondering why Kaylee was so eager to hold onto me while

Margery remained distant, and where would I sleep, alone in my cramped tent somewhere in the dark? My gear was at Kaylee's place.

For the moment, however, I was energized by my surroundings and motivated by my unanswered questions—"Kaylee," I said but she didn't respond. With the exception of her sudden bursts of affection or confusion, she had become increasingly withdrawn since meeting her on the trail with Josh, what seemed like a long time ago now—but had only been what? Two days?

"Where's Josh?" I asked.

"Josh?" she responded innocently. As if she didn't know.

Margery took my hand and leaned close, and whispered in my ear, "Not now."

I turned to her and felt an agonizing attraction, our planets ready to collide and create a cataclysmic explosion. I wanted to touch her, to feel forever connected and embracing, yet—I couldn't.

"Where," I asked, "should I stay tonight?"

"Where you like."

"With you."

"You can sleep at my house."

My mind raced into fantasies of our bodies entwined on her bed beneath an open window full of stars, but the tone of her voice made me suspect she was thinking more coolly. The three of us walked unconnected but together and we were soon at Kaylee's.

"Are you okay?" Margery asked her. "Do you want me to stay with you tonight?"

So that was her plan. I could have her place while she stayed and took care of Kaylee … but Kaylee said no, and they hugged and I took advantage of what might be an extended parting to rush inside and grab my pack, heavy, its familiar damp earth smell, essential, and lugged it past Kaylee, hugged her briefly and eased away. Soon Kaylee was inside and Margery and I were together alone and instead of feeling relieved I felt suddenly tense—full of burning questions with no easy way to ask them.

"So?" I said.

"I have a pullout."

"A what?"

"An extra bed."

Margery

"Okay," I said and then rushed on awkwardly and bluntly, never one to know how to ask a delicate question. "What's with Kaylee?"

My pack hung loosely on my shoulders—and we walked in the dark, me struggling to keep my mouth shut while waiting forever for her to answer, and just when I thought she was going to ignore me completely, we stopped at her front porch and she turned toward me.

"Nothing," she said.

At first, I wasn't sure what she was referring to—had she actually said, "Nothing?" Did she even speak at all, the word itself floating into the dark air as a perpetual ultimate answer? Or was it an auditory hallucination?

"We're all fine," she said.

I recalled a joke from my days in an office, a coworker making fun of a high-strung boss who always told us she was *fine*. F.I.N.E. for frightened, insecure, nervous, and emotional. But it didn't apply to Margery. She didn't stress the word. She spoke with a calm finality that made the joke irrelevant.

After helping her yank out a bed from a dusty, clanging couch pushed against the front window, and tossing my pack onto it, we went to her kitchen, my appetite returning as she pulled out a bowl of melon and strawberries, so juicy and sweet, a little tart, and we ate quietly together like old friends while I imagined her touch, and a sequence of events that would lead me into her bedroom. But I remained puzzled by Josh's disappearance and Kaylee's odd attraction to me, a misplaced desire, and Margery's lack of desire, and I wanted to rearrange the universe.

She got up, and as she receded away from me down the hallway to her room, I felt a twang of abandonment, as if she was leaving never to return, yet we hadn't even kissed.

There was nothing I could do but attend to my own functions, brushing my teeth and carefully avoiding any rigorous brushing of my broken molar. I washed my face and glanced in the small mirror—almost aghast at what a character I'd become—weathered, bearded, dirty—the mirror was small with worn silver streaks, but even so, and even though I'd bathed in cold streams, a shower seemed like a good idea—and since this small coffin-sized half-bath with dark wood walls had no shower, I envisioned sneaking down the hall to Margery's room and showering with her. Our skin would be rough and slightly sagging together but we would transcend bodily decay. I shook the idea rattling around in my head, and decided that it sounded like marijuana talk—something I might say while extremely high.

I stripped down and washed my face and arms, down my legs, in every crack and pore and went naked into the front room where I dug around in my pack, finding clothes that were not quite as dirty as what I'd been wearing, clothes soiled early in my trip that now seemed relatively clean. I pulled on undergarments, pattered back to the bathroom mirror and bared my teeth like a chimp making sure they were absolutely clean, worried about an infection; face clean but still weathered and scraggly, graying beard, overgrown eyebrows, ears needing a trim and eyes bloodshot, and I told myself to avoid mirrors.

Settling into the creaking bed felt good, surprisingly comfortable and warm—often my thermal ground pad was more comfortable than an old bed—and I lay there enjoying the night, able to see a few stars out the front window, imagining Margery's body next to mine.

Sometime in the night I woke with a start—something about having sex with Margery, who then turned into someone like Kaylee, emaciated, and then distant howling—none of it real except the howling, which could have been coyotes or merely the wind, but I felt compelled to find out for sure so I rolled out of the creaking bed, pulled on my shorts and shoes, and opened the front door, shivering in my T-shirt, stepping out onto the porch and into the cool, almost frosty air, common for those morning hours long before sunrise. The howling had subsided, but now there was a faint grumbling sound with an odd intermittent cadence. I felt drawn, the rhythmic pace sounding like perpetually unintelligible conversation. Moving slowly into sight was a white nightgown, ghostly in the frosty air, Jackie walking barefoot down the road, speaking into the night, and as I stepped toward her, trying to understand her words, she saw me and said, "Who are you?"

I introduced myself as her dinner guest and she began cussing at me with a vindictive flurry of profanity the likes of which I hadn't heard since my wife and I got into a fierce argument when we were in our twenties, a battle so irreversible it changed the course of our relationship.

I stared at Jackie, this ghost woman screaming at me in the night, and saw a tracking device around her ankle, a green light blinking on,

Margery

and off, on with each repetition of a cussword, synchronized with her fury, spittle flinging in the starlight and her body leaning forward, arms rigidly at her sides, brow furrowed, and my astonishment quickly turned to a sort of admiration for this fiery woman who had lived a long full life and now found herself standing alone in the dark, tracked like a criminal—maybe she was but I doubted it—fighting against everything that was wrong with her world at this moment, and I had become what was wrong.

Suddenly, she fell silent and floated away toward the stream—was she going to throw herself in? I stood watching, amazed, and wondering what I should, or should not do. Fortunately, Henry arrived, walking fast but stiffly, as if he'd just been roused. "Hello Jeremy, pleasant morning ... I see Jackie's going for a swim."

"Looks like it."

As he rushed past, following her, he said, "She gets a bit agitated."

I got the impression he didn't want my help, but I waited for awhile to see if they'd come back this way, then my whole body shuddered against the cold and I retreated inside.

It took me until dawn—gray light seeping in the windows—to doze off, and wake much later to the sound of Margery clanking pans. And the smell of coffee and steel-cut oatmeal steaming from a bowl, blueberries on top, and I was greeted in the kitchen by Margery's tired eyes and close-lipped, almost sad smile, and I wondered if this was another bungee jump day—did she jump every day like people showered and brushed their teeth? She nodded at me when I thanked her for the oatmeal and blueberries and she watched me eat. I finished half before noticing she wasn't eating. I had assumed she'd join me.

She grabbed a handful of blueberries, drank a thick green juice, and sipped coffee. The coffee helped both our spirits—to an extent—my body always felt stiff and beaten in the morning. With the caffeine charge, my curiosity boiled to the surface.

I wanted to know about Jackie and, at the same time, did not want to know—I was afraid of potential anguish, afraid that my empathy might destroy me. One thing I knew conclusively—whatever her trouble, I could do nothing about it. I lacked the means to do anything other than blunder about the wilderness. Call it selective intelligence or willful ignorance, denial or being an ass, but I chose to know nothing. I sometimes actively sought stupor. I'm not proud of it, and I know that such ignorance can spawn bloody rituals, fanaticism, extremism, insanity. It was a fine line—my thoughts and feelings shaping my reality—*be happy man!* If you can believe your way to happiness, then you can just as easily believe your way to misery. It might be difficult for me to enjoy life if I knew too much about Jackie. So, the less I knew the better.

Josh, on the other hand, was a lost young man, or missing or something, and maybe I could help find him, or help him find himself, or so I thought, and accepted that Kaylee's affection toward me was very likely transference of some sort—I was a stand-in for Josh. So where was he?

Margery remained a conundrum, but I could help Josh.

I'd finished my breakfast and was clearing the dishes when I formulated a simple yet more calculated question. "How well do you know Josh?"

Margery looked at me as if she knew exactly what I had in mind, her eyes fully upon me for what felt like the first time, her close-lipped smile puzzling and alluring, and I felt another sudden urge to hold onto her, but she must have sensed my attraction, and she moved away, around the kitchen counter, attending to a useless chore, wiping down a clean counter top.

"I haven't seen him …" I said, waiting, expecting her to fill in an explanation. Nothing. So I repeated the more direct question. "Where is he?"

She leaned against the counter and stared. "I don't know."

"Wasn't he Kaylee's … friend?" And I congratulated myself on my tact.

"They're married."

"Married?" Don't know why it surprised me. Maybe because there were no rings, but then, I never wore my own wedding ring, mainly because it was dangerous when rock climbing—rings could get caught on things—I've seen pictures of fingers torn off by wedding rings. I got used to not wearing mine. But Josh and Kaylee were so young. A false assumption—young relative to me maybe, but not so young for marriage. In fact, it's likely I was married at their age.

Margery disappeared into her bedroom while I stood looking out the front window, wondering what to do, and she returned wearing

Margery

polyurethane shorts and a snug black top, athletic looking and determined, maybe a bit frenzied. She opened the front door.

"You're jumping?" I asked, surprised by my own incredulity.

She paused but then hurried out and I chased after her as she practically ran toward the cliff. I grabbed her arm. She turned, eyes fierce, hawk-like as if I were trying to stop a force of nature. I met her angry eyes, mine showing fear, not as prey, but as someone else, someone who felt compelled to be with her forever even if it meant leaping to my own death. "I would," I said evenly, letting go, "feel better if you didn't."

Margery softened, shook her head and said, "You're just like Josh."

I stood bewildered as she turned away, disappearing into the woods, clearly headed for the stream-crossing and another climb to the top of the cliff.

7

IT WAS ONLY A FEW DAYS AGO that I met Josh and Kaylee, seeing Josh standing in the smaller stream, on the other side of the eastern ridge, and I again felt my envy at his youth—clearly that's what it was—and now I wanted to help him? Did I want to make sure he got everything he could from his life because I had not? Wasn't that how the old always felt about the young, and didn't the angst of youth recede into insignificance only when confronted by the realities of age? Was I like Josh when I was younger? Maybe. Or did we remain essentially the same, holding onto our pettiness and fear, or worse, our bigotry and false assumptions, hardening along with our arteries? But there appeared to be something more immediate implied in Margery's comparison. What was it?

I followed her, the ascent easier now that I'd done it once already, knowing the path, when to conserve, when to reach for a hand hold. Margery never looked back to see me tailing her, but surely she knew. She had acute senses, an awareness that permeated far beyond her immediate surroundings. Soon we were atop the cliff, and she was preparing for her death, or so I imagined. She pulled up her bungee cord and coiled it at her feet near the edge, an updraft lifting her cropped hair, and trees below

Margery

waving their leaves to and fro, green and light green, surface and underside, back and forth like goodbye.

"Margery."

She tightened the black harness around her waist, then strapped the cord around her strong ankle, her legs athletic and arms muscular, thin but strong, and I sensed her determination wavering. I had a chance. I stepped closer as she stood on the edge.

She looked into the clear sky. "Are you going to come along this time?"

I wasn't sure how to respond—I'd always enjoyed scaling mountain peaks and some easy rock walls but never leaping from them—only an amusement park jump that was exhilarating and terrifying. I looked at her anchor—the blue webbing the same as yesterday, when she'd sailed out far enough to miss the protruding rock.

She bent down and touched the blue webbing. "I can move this." She sounded hopeful, and I must've given her pause, because she proceeded to rearrange the jump, making it less dangerous.

Then she stood facing me, eyes boring into me, challenging me. "Come on," she said.

Was she daring me to leap off the cliff with her? On the same cord? I was clearly not ready to leap to my death—what I felt for her must have been nothing more than romantic hyperbole at its worst. Wasn't it?

"The weight," I said as if reason would win out and she would immediately see that the cord would snap or that the trajectory would be thrown off and we'd crash into the cliff, or we'd stretch to the bottom of the stream and break our necks. Both of us would be killed or worse—maimed and suffering.

"Yes, the weight," she said. "This will change things."

Of course it would; it would change all sorts of things. Margery was insane. No way I could justify jumping with her—she looked at me, must have known what I was thinking, waved at me sarcastically and went over the edge like stepping off the side of a swimming pool.

I felt miserable. Despite taking the sane approach, I felt like a coward. And I was angry, mostly at Margery for putting me in that position. Now I had to climb down to see if she survived yet again, as surely she had, especially because she'd done this "safe" jump, alone, so many times that it was routine, but anything could happen, and probably would at some point because she had a death wish and likely didn't check her equipment often and likely it would fail eventually, one too many pulls against the serrated rock—such were my thoughts as I descended, always peering down looking for some sign of Margery, and scrambled across the stream where the water boiled white over boulders.

Things had changed. By not jumping, my relationship with Margery, such as it had been, had shifted from adoration and infatuation to madness and anger and a fleeting wish to find her smashed against the rocks so I could feel selfishly vindicated—the absurdity of me standing over her corpse telling her I told you so. A sober reminder of the insanity and depth of my feelings for her.

I took the path downstream, my anger subsiding to a smolder not quite extinguished, easily flamed if I wasn't careful, and neared the clearing where Margery's cord usually hung and where she might normally emerge from the water like a resurrected goddess, and found nothing. I squinted, looking for the cord, searching for Margery or Margery's body—*come on*, I thought, *at least the bungee cord must be there*. She couldn't have ascended the cliff again, on some secret path, and pulled the cord back up—the only other explanation was that the cord had finally snapped and Margery had succeeded in killing herself, which must have been her intent all along.

I stood at the water's edge, the clear deep stream, the amber stones rising up to the bank and the ripples changing it all into a dream—and my anger gave way to sorrow and an immense sense of loss, and I felt like throwing myself into the cold water and swimming deep to find her, joining her in the eternal depths.

I didn't of course. I steeled myself against it, and clung to self-preservation, as I had learned to do for most of my life—having learned long ago that essentially I and only I was responsible for my life and happiness, my sadness and misery. It was a lesson useful only at times like these, and often a lesson needing to be unlearned when absorbed in the warmth of friends and family, or in the complex interconnectedness of my surroundings—in this case, the town, eternity.

Why was I angry? Had I any right to be? I studied the striated rock face, the ledges, bulges, the small bushes here and there, and having

Margery

shed my love-anger conflagration, I could logically conclude that the cord may have bounced back up upon release and gotten hung up somewhere—so I carefully scanned back and forth, finally finding it draped over a branch not all that far from the water, just where you might expect, easy to see once you've seen it.

So where was she? Was she hiding in the bushes watching to see if I would break down and cry about her—was her intent to inflict pain? Or was this some sick joke perpetuated to test my resolve or to reveal my intentions? Fed up with the possibility that it was a test or game, I decided once again that it was time for me to leave, perhaps with greater resolve this time. I was standing not far from the pile of rocks we'd heaved onto George's shallow grave, and felt as if George could grab me and happily pull me under. I wanted to avoid that.

Then suddenly my jaw throbbed—I'd been clenching my teeth and must've irritated my bad tooth. I touched my jaw, almost imperceptibly swollen, swelling more with my touch, and panicked at the thought of enduring constant pain—thus exacerbating it, having to remind myself that I could exert some self-control and assure myself it would pass—on the other hand, it might need some dental attention.

So George the dentist had reached me from the grave, hadn't he?

I looked toward the cliff and wondered if there was a way out that direction. Was there a trail that led west to the peaks and beyond? Should I go that way? But what if I hiked deep into the wilderness and my tooth rotted and got infected and I was pulled into the earth by something as absurd as a broken molar? Or should I return the way I had come? Things were always different going the other direction. And perhaps going back isn't the same as going backwards.

I stepped onto Margery's porch, calling her name. I went inside, called her again, going from room to room, then checked the contents of my backpack. Everything appeared to be there—the stove, the last of my food, tent—but why expect anything to be missing? Had I been more trusting than usual and now was I back to being hyper-alert? Had Margery done that to me, or was I just naturally reverting to my perpetual state of self-preservation?

It was past noon when I emerged from Margery's house, my backpack weighing me down with my decision to escape, and that guy in his sweats was jogging heavily past, and a few others milled about, aimlessly it seemed—or were they carefree?—then I saw the hiking group on an afternoon hike toward the northern peaks, impenetrable mountains I'd wanted to explore before taking this detour into this unmarked town between the two streams that converged forming a river cascading down the valley. The group waved cheerfully at me, most using hiking poles, keeping steady on level ground and no doubt keeping them from stumbling into oblivion when they climbed higher. Who knew how far they'd go? Maybe they'd only stroll through the forest a short way and look at birds or watch the leaves dance in the afternoon sunlight—some looked barely capable of walking, shorts revealing swollen veins, discolored blotches on sagging skin, thick ankles and loose joints—others lean and muscular and seemingly young, if not for the gray hair and the preponderance of spectacles.

But they were jovial and, in the eight or so of them, I recognized several, those hikers I'd met already. This time, I wanted to stop them and ask them questions, and socialize with them, if only to find Margery, not ready yet to launch myself alone again into the unknown, wanting as we all do, to be with others, and as my anger at Margery subsided, the compelling force to leave her and the town also subsided. So I wasn't going to give up on her quite so easily. But before I could rouse myself to stop the hikers, they began filing onto a relatively narrow trail. While watching them disappear into the woods, I hadn't noticed Kaylee in the road ahead.

"Hi Kaylee," I said, forcing my voice calm but failing miserably. "Where's Margery? I mean, have you seen her? Do you know where she is?"

Kaylee stared at me and her face again was droopy and oddly figured, and I thought she must have had a stroke, but she was so young and it seemed so out of place and unlikely that I tried ignoring it and again focused on her brown eyes, big and beautiful—mainly because of their affection. But even they seemed dim today.

"Kaylee?"

"Oh," she responded. "It's you."

"Yes," I said, "hello."

"Where's Josh?" she asked.

Margery

She sounded coherent—her voice clear, no slurring, but why would she think I knew where Josh went? I replied stupidly, maybe a little caustic. "How the hell should I know?" And regretted it immediately when she cringed as if I'd slapped her.

"He left," she said, then stared at my pack, "And you're leaving too?"

What was it with these people? I'd come to the wilderness to be alone, to escape such entrapments, and here so easily I'd been drawn into the world of human emotions—empathy, joy, sympathy and anger and madness.

"I don't know," I said, "Didn't get far. I'm still here. Talking to you. Looking for Margery."

"She loves you."

I stared hard into Kaylee's eyes—what the hell did that mean? And what about her, Kaylee, and her hugs? What was that? Was I a Josh substitute? Or a father figure? Why were these people out to destroy me and my quest for solitude and peace? So Margery supposedly loved me? So much that she wanted me to join her in a ridiculous lover's leap? Screw that. I'm a survivor.

Suddenly Kaylee grimaced, put her hand to her neck and rubbed and wobbled like she might fall, so I slipped out of my pack and held her arm. Then she relaxed and looked at me, "I'll be all right." She forced a smile. "Josh said he believed in me, but now he's gone and I'm alone—will you hold me just for a minute? Then I've got to see Doctor Henry."

Of course I held her. How could I not? And my heart melted for her and I reconsidered my envy of Josh's youthful vitality—it appeared it was accompanied by cold-hearted selfishness—how could he leave Kaylee? I was forced to confront my own youth—routinely saying and doing unpleasant things without much regard for their effect on others. Had I been like Josh?

Kaylee held onto me like she'd never let go, and this time, at least for me, it encompassed so much more than the fleeting desire to become young like her; it represented my deepest tragic flaw and threat to my own self-preservation, the desire to uplift humanity itself, to allow all the Kaylees of the world to live a long, glorious, and prosperous life, a desire that doomed me to catastrophic failure and thus my need to suppress it, to avoid being pulled into the earth like George, avoid leaping off a cliff with Margery. So I could continue my ultimate quest for self—leaving me perpetually alone in the wilderness.

"Come on," I said, "I'll help you."

The afternoon sun was making its way west toward the cliff and the sky remained bright blue except for a few cumulus clouds in the east, stark white, pink around the edges. Kaylee and I walked with my arm around her shoulder as she leaned into me, almost fused hip to hip and synchronized in our step, our bodies moving together toward Doctor Henry's home. The doctor appeared out front and when he saw us, he seemed immediately to know something—as if he'd been expecting this sight, someone helping Kaylee to his door, for weeks, maybe even months, obviously long before I'd arrived.

"Hello Kaylee," he said, ignoring me, not acknowledging my help, which was odd, and at the same time oddly selfish of me to feel slighted.

He took Kaylee's hand and arm and I released her to the doctor, who still did not acknowledge me, leaving me standing alone outside. I had left my backpack again unattended, this time abandoned in the dirt on the side of the road. I was ready to go back and retrieve it when Margery appeared in the doorway. "Are you joining us?" she asked. She wore a long cotton dress, blue and yellow, and her hair was tangled and partially wet, gray and brown, giving her a natural shape tinged with concern.

She was so stunningly beautiful to me at that moment that whatever ill feelings she might have foisted upon me were erased, at least from my immediate memory, dispelled by her beauty—not a classical, traditional, or even androgynous twenty-first century beauty—but an intimate, wholly personal beauty that felt designed not necessarily by her but by nature itself, intended for me only, and only for that moment. It was too much for me to assimilate as my heart at once flooded with longing for her, then froze in fear. *Would I join them? In what?*

8

THE DOCTOR AND MARGERY were there and two others, neither of which I recalled seeing in town before now—an older man clearly in his descending years but with a steady gaze and a strong grip as I shook his hand and he introduced himself merely as a friend, no name and leaving me comfortably with the feeling that no names were needed—and a woman seemingly of the same age, maybe older, who radiated good cheer and health and who took my hand with both of hers, smiled, and exuded warmth despite the faint smell of an epoch, an amalgam of garlic, sage, and chocolate, and she wouldn't let go of my hand—yet I felt comfortable holding it as if we were long lost lovers strolling through the park romanticizing about our full, fun-filled lives. She was describing her childhood home as if we'd both been raised there and she led me through the dining room, the others following, out to a back screened-in porch that had a breathtaking view through the trees, open sky stretching out over the gorge to the valley.

In the center of the porch was an elevated bed, a single-wide bed that seemed more like a table or a slab of thick concrete made up with a pillow and covers, and Kaylee stood at the head of this slab-bed, her face

Margery

contorted, misshapen, her natural beauty concealed by fear. The epochal woman pulled me near the bed and I felt myself tense—was this some sort of bizarre trick? They were going to strap me down, perform a grotesque ritual on me, carve out my brain, offer it to the mountain gods, or eat it, or transplant it? But, as my fears heightened with each leap of my destructive imagination, so too did the woman's grip tighten, as if to counteract my fears—or to keep me from running—and she asked me inane questions about my hobbies, suddenly shifting to questions about my desire to be alone, and my feelings for Margery—all so perfectly reasonable and natural. I gazed across the strange slab of bed, Margery on the other side glancing at me—but I was unable to gain her full attention. I felt she might somehow be disappointed in me. She looked away and we all watched Doctor Henry approach Kaylee and give her something—was it something to eat? Was it like the Holy Ghost, the Eucharist, those tasteless wafers? Kaylee was the only recipient and she chewed and then, helped by Doctor Henry, she lay on the slab-bed-table and the rest of us circled her, ready to assist I suppose—in what, I was still unclear about, but as the next hour or so passed, I formulated some fairly accurate theories—recalling what went on during my youth—drug experiments—teenage friends on acid, and watching one of them panic and nearly kill himself trying to run away from giant spiders chasing him across a suburban golf course while the rest of us laughed uproariously and he tumbled down the back side of a steeply elevated precisely manicured putting green into a tree, breaking his collarbone and arm, then screaming so loudly that the rest of us fled in panic, returning only after we battled the Viet Cong swarming down the fairway, playing war like I did when a child with my brother now long dead from alcoholism. Our teenager friend was unconscious when we dragged him back up the slope and tumbled him into a golf cart, then a car, dumping him out on his parents' front lawn, ringing the doorbell and running. Maybe our actions then could have been explained by the whiskey—or maybe the synthetic acid was tainted with other artificial enhancers bad for us, but on the whole, it was a trip most unlike what I was witnessing with Kaylee as she lay comfortably on the raised slab bed and we stood around her, reassuring her, every action for her benefit, selfless giving that enriched the self—only I, it appeared, held back, positioning myself where I would be least likely to be needed, at the foot of the bed, making me more of an observer than a participant or helper.

Margery held Kaylee's hand close to her chest while Kaylee spoke—the words hanging in the air magically and easy for me to remember because of their intensity—in fact, I have trouble forgetting them. In the midst of bizarre descriptions of wildlife more suitable to a planet other than earth, she became quiet and tranquil, and then she spoke calmly and clearly in the candlelight and diffuse starlight.

"It all makes so much sense now. Yes. So simple and so beautiful."

Whatever she was experiencing made sense to her but was agonizingly frustrating to me—what? What made sense? How? She could describe purple monkeys, insects shaped like musical instruments, and gold rivers of air, but in her moment of clarity, this was all she had to say?

Margery and the others were attentive while Kaylee described what she was "seeing" with her closed eyes—or more accurately, hallucinating—but then I wondered if there was any difference. Everyone seemed calm and suffused with acceptance, embracing the reality of the hallucinations and covering that reality in some sort of love.

By the end of the two or more hours, I was allowing my cynicism to creep in, and Kaylee's utterances took on the form of a New Age silliness that I'd mocked occasionally over the years. Not that I hadn't at least technically embraced some of the concepts and the techniques—meditation, mindfulness, exercise, yoga, real food—but often New Age groups seemed to mimic hippie communes, and before that, the beats and bohemians and so on, and in mimicry came pretension. In trying so hard to avoid pretension, however, I sometimes became someone who I was not, and often aborted someone I could have been.

Kaylee was helped to her feet, and I helped Doctor Henry and the healthy elderly woman move the bed out of the way, and then we all set out snacks and drinks—lots of water, but including alcohol—and mingled as if at a cocktail party.

Kaylee looked like she'd just scaled Everest and returned, still alive but changed immeasurably, no longer anxious, serenity descending upon her as she excitedly talked about her experience, how she'd met family members long gone, and Josh—she said goodbye to him with some sadness but understood his fear—she wished him the best and hoped he could avoid feeling guilty—she couldn't find words to describe everything she'd seen, as if words were blunt instruments incapable of adequately describing her hallucinogenic mountain climb.

I drank gin over ice—the wine-and-cannabis-infused meal was excellent, but I still enjoyed the sometimes-precise numbing effect of hard alcohol. The group of hikers arrived and joined the others inside—they looked more or less happy—some clearly pushing themselves beyond their capability, straining to have fun when they should have been resting.

I avoided asking direct questions—preferring to say things like "That was interesting," hoping someone would fill in the details, but they didn't—they seemed intent on forcing me to commit, wanting me to reveal my insecurities through anxious inquiry, but I held firm—see how smart I was?

Margery had stepped outside onto the deck and was leaning against the railing when I joined her, and we stood side by side in a cool evening breeze, the view enthralling, the ridge tapering away and joining the gorge opening up to the valley beyond, and the cliff. I sipped my gin. I tried to formulate an intelligent question about the—ceremony? Party?

"What," I asked, "was that all about?"

She leaned against the railing and gazed at the view, presumably as captivated as I was—but maybe not; likely, she'd seen it before. "You know already," she said.

Then I blurted out something I normally would have had enough sense to calculate, "What I know is that you left me alone on that cliff and just disappeared."

"Disappeared?"

I felt foolish, and finished my gin looking over my shoulder and thinking about leaving her, at least for the moment, to get another gin. I rolled ice around my tongue and felt it clunk against my molar.

Margery seemed to take pity on me. She touched my arm and I flinched, but then calmed as if her touch was everything I'd ever wanted in the world, even though all touch was fleeting, and gaining what I wanted only ensured the subsequent ache of missing what I once had.

"Ask me," she said.

I stared at her, her blue eyes, crow's feet, short hair, and wanted to know if she had said something to Kaylee and if so, was it true. But I was a coward, even at an age where honesty should come more easily, and I felt like a failure. Had I not matured at all? Then another thought suddenly intruded. Where was Doctor Henry's wife—the wandering ghost of a woman with the ankle bracelet—where had she been while we were "socializing"?

I glanced over my shoulder to look for Jackie, knowing of course she wasn't there, but using the gesture as a preface to my question, a level of pretension I used quite naturally. "Where's Jackie?"

Margery smiled at me, like she'd made a bet and bluffed her way to a win. "Asleep," she said.

"No wonder," I said, "she wanders around all night." Normally, at cocktail parties, I'd expect a laugh, as I meant to be witty, but this one fell flat.

"She's going fast," Margery said.

"Where?"

Margery obliged me with a chuckle, then said, "You already know that one too. You just don't want to know."

"Can you blame me?"

"No one here wants to blame anyone for anything."

And so you can't blame me, even now, for not wanting to describe the intricacies and the details of the disease that had gripped Jackie and driven her into the night searching for what? Herself? Her essence? Searching for the memories she'd lost, for her childhood, for the last shreds of her life now dissolving? Or was she merely looking for her next step—a cold swim at night in white water crashing over boulders?

I again glanced over my shoulder, this time knowing that when Jackie woke, which would be soon, she might be cheerful for awhile and repeat what she knew about her world, but would eventually sink into anxiety and despair and might go screaming into the forest—was it all that different than my own sojourns into the wilderness?

And then I thought I'd better make good use of my time while Margery was being open and generous.

"And Josh?" I asked. "What happened with him?"

"Nobody knows where he went but the 'where' isn't important. He left his wife Kaylee because he couldn't bear it any longer. Did he love her too much or not enough? Maybe it would've killed him, or he

Margery

thought it would have. Some people aren't able to ..." She trailed off, perhaps in deference to my own anxieties.

"Kaylee?" I said. "She's dying?"

Margery looked at me, her eyes steady and she nodded. In the cold reality of the moment, my feelings for her lacked passion and focus. I was adrift, detached, then fully consumed by uncertainty that could only be relieved by knowledge, while simultaneously driven to avoid knowing anything—what did I need to know to survive alone in the forest, in the mountains where I was headed before being sidetracked by this impossible community?

I had suspected something had gone horribly wrong in Kaylee's relationship with Josh, but dismissed it as a mere quarrel, exacerbated by his departure, but I had not thought, consciously anyway, that she was dying. Did I need to know what was killing her? Not really. It wouldn't alleviate my overwhelming sadness. And again, I was not smart enough to help. *This,* I thought, *is why I avoid crowds.*

I took a moment to reflect on the ceremony or ritual or whatever it was—therapy?

"So," I asked, "the doctor gave Kaylee what? LSD?"

"Psilocybin."

"To ease her anxiety?" I asked with profound incredulity, recalling my own experiences.

"Yes, we've found that under the right therapeutic circumstances, it can help with the process, sometimes even reduce the anxiety enough to send some disease into remission or hold it back for years ..."

"Okay," I said. "I get it." Again not wanting too many details, and ignoring her use of "we" because, while it made my admiration for Margery increase, it also came with potentially unsettling implications. "So the hallucinations ... they fool her into thinking it's not a big deal."

"Something like that, I suppose. We don't really know for sure. How can we?"

Again with the "we," I thought, and was about ready to make some dumb joke, trying mightily to deflect reality. "So it's therapy." My next question never made it into the air, as perhaps I feared it the most. Did she love me? Why would Kaylee say she did?

"Anything else?" Margery asked.

What I did then bothers me still now, or maybe it's what I didn't do—I did not respond. I stared at her and got lost in all the complexities that invariably come with tossing around the word "love." I loved beer and the mountains and I loved my old beat-up backpack—and then I remembered I'd left it on the side of the road near Kaylee's house. Was that any way to treat something you loved?

Margery was waiting patiently, watching me hesitate. The shadows from the western cliff had covered the town, but the yellowing aspen on the eastern ridge remained washed bright in sunlight.

Then I heard Jackie yelling angrily behind us, "Henry! Why did you let me sleep so late? Are you having a party without me! Is that what you're doing?" Jackie stood at the doorway to the porch, her hair long, white and wild, her green robe wrapped tightly around her, her face pretty but flushed red, and it was as if her anger was struggling to transform itself into a joke, her unyielding will trying to force herself into cheerfulness and sociability.

The others surrounded her, taking turns trying to reassure her, successful just long enough to allow the next person to try a different approach, then slowly filing out, saying goodbye and saying thanks to Henry—Kaylee lingering and waving at Margery—and Margery excused herself from me, the two of them slipping away into the evening, leaving me alone, which was no surprise to me because I often acted as if I wanted to be alone.

Inside, I heard Jackie's anger take control again, Jackie berating the world while Henry tried to steer the conversation deep into a past I clearly knew nothing about. I escaped by leaping over the deck railing, the incline much steeper than expected, twisting my ankle and sliding down the rock and dirt slope onto the next road over, and wandered in the shadows passing what appeared to be George's house, which must have also served as his office, the wooden sign saying simply—Dentist—and by that mere association my broken molar suddenly throbbed, and I worried it might become seriously infected, enough to kill me.

"Stop!" I yelled, and looked around to see if anyone had heard, then made my way back to Kaylee's and found my pack in the brush, just as I'd left it. I heaved it onto my back, looked up at the eastern ridge

Margery

turning red and felt the coolness of the evening—the gin had worn off and I shivered.

All I wanted was to be warm. That was the appeal of being alone in the mountains. Everything was reduced to its simplest forms—food, shelter, warmth—no complications. But I didn't want to camp in the road, nor did I necessarily want to start hiking up the ridge and end up hiking in the dark, usually not a good idea.

So I stood alone, hungry, waiting for someone, anyone really, to appear from nowhere and invite me in for dinner, as the few people here must be gathering around a table and eating food that made you feel alive and ready for another day—one more day of my life and one more day than yesterday. And the cannabis-infused cookies—yes, that sounded good.

I stared at Kaylee's front porch, wondering if Margery was still with her, torn, unsure about banging on the front door and inviting myself in, perhaps as an unwanted guest—if they had wanted me, wouldn't they have asked?

Standing alone in the empty road, staring at a closed door wondering if people were having fun and living a good life without me, made me want to run away. In the desperation common to all evenings, when the setting sun marked the alacrity of time passing, my mind churned with threatening possibilities, my thoughts congealing around Margery and my exposed heart.

I analyzed my attraction to, my friendship, my short-lived familiarity with the woman who threw herself off cliffsides with the abandon of someone who thought she was immortal, and the more I reduced our relationship to semantics, descriptions befitting what I might have in common with any human being, the easier it was for me to turn away from her.

Pivoting and ignoring my twisted ankle, I hiked swiftly with new resolve toward the ridge and the trail from which I'd come—if I could find it. With my movement, I was more decisive—with movement came momentum—and I would flee this odd, lively town, filled with death, get outside of this strange basin and return to my own life, where death had the decency to hide in the alleyways and behind newscasts where I could ignore it, only occasionally having to beat it away. The daily news was merely entertainment, nothing real, nothing that touched my life. I was lying to myself of course—the world I would return to was comforting only because of its familiarity and my ability to create routines as a barrier against the daily onslaught of bad news.

I hiked to the edge of town where I had emerged several days ago—seemed so much longer—and searched for the way out, some indication of a trail, a footpath, having completely ignored it on the way in, which was unusual for me because I usually marked my way out, or at least made mental note—I had ventured into many gloomy forests over the years and learned to mark my exit, but not this time.

While concerned, there was no reason to believe I couldn't emerge from the wilderness within a day or two—bushwhack to the ridge top, get my bearings, cross the eastern stream where I'd first seen Josh, and make my way to the wide trail that led back to the endless congestion between mountains and big city, a bustling community where I'd been somewhat successful but had become disillusioned, where the brown clouds of auto exhaust melded with my own exhaustion and hovered perpetually over the steel, brick, and polyurethane, the fiber optic walled fortress of downtown where I had planned to go next to visit an old friend—someone who knew my wife and kids when we were young. That's the sort of thing people did.

9

I STARTED UP THE RIDGE, through the brush, past trees, some thick and gnarled, others fallen, climbing over them, the terrain challenging and ever ascending—only one direction to go and I felt the joy of knowing that going up would eventually get me there, get me to a point where the sky meets the earth and I might find momentary peace.

Gravity pulled hard at me as I kept pushing higher on steep slopes through the darkening forest. I arrived at that massive rock slab where we'd stopped on the way in and felt my confidence surge—the path was somewhere on the upside of that rock and I would be home free, but the only remaining light came from the highest point, the highest tree atop the ridge, a spear dipped in blood, lit red by the setting sun. If I pushed on, I would crest the top of the ridge in the dark and would have to climb that spear tip to see the stars and the moon. While I'd found that sort of joy and exhilaration before, this time the effort of climbing a tree at night felt dangerous and unnecessary, especially since the rock slab already created an open area with an excellent view.

The air was chilling rapidly as I unrolled my tent onto the only flat surface, one side hugging the rock, the other touching the steep incline.

Margery

I pulled on warm clothes and sat exhausted, back against the rock, shoveling in the last of my gorp, chewing, crunching—a nut coming down hard onto my cracked molar, and I let out a yelp, then spoke to the woods, "You idiot."

Self-affirmation, I thought, wearily. I was an idiot but was too tired to list all the reasons—I shivered and unzipped the tent opening and lay on my back with my head sticking out, a meal for the mosquitoes, my skin a sweet glaze, and stared at the stars as I often did, looking for answers, and listened to a mosquito buzzing, and go quiet, and then a loud ringing in my ear after I hit myself in an attempt to kill the mosquito, while another sucked blood from my forehead.

At least I was warm enough, but with the warmth, there was no way to escape my thoughts and emotions, and in a way, I was thankful for the distraction of the mosquitoes. I withdrew to the safety of my coffin-sized tent, killed three unlucky enough to sneak inside, bloody smears, then lay awake staring into the darkness, wishing I'd stolen a few of those cannabis cookies.

My thoughts started to gain their own life, and while I enjoyed being alone, I didn't enjoy those times when my thoughts wouldn't allow me to be truly alone. I questioned myself, again—what the hell was I doing? Why was I headed back to where I'd come from, where technological experts might prolong my life a few years? Unlike Margery, who experienced a sort of immortality by ignoring her own mortality. Is that what she was doing? What bold thoughts allowed her to throw herself off a cliff?

This thinking quickly had me scrounging around my gear, desperately searching my pack for the last sleeping pill that I knew must be there somewhere. This time no nibbling. I was going to eat the whole pill, and if by chance there was another one, I'd eat that one too—Ambien, the sort of pharmaceutical I could fully appreciate. I found some crumbs and white powder in a sandwich bag and licked the plastic, and kept looking for more.

Then I heard something outside, a branch snapping, then another, and then a cascading group of sounds—branches, rocks tumbling and cracking like firecrackers and sailing off into woods, pebbles pinging and bouncing off my tent.

I knew the sound of wildlife in the woods and immediately knew that this was human wildlife, a person crashing through the night down the slope and falling nearby with a thud and a groan. I climbed from my tent, flashlight in hand, and shined it on someone at my feet, about to roll further down until I grabbed his shoulder, and he looked up at me shielding his eyes. Josh, haggard and beaten, only a small day pack attached to his back like a deformity, his lips dry and cracked and his face sweat-streaked with dirt.

He screamed, "Leave me alone!"

"Josh," I said, "It's me … you know, Jeremy …"

"I don't care. Let me go!"

"You'll hurt yourself. Slow down. Let me help."

Josh glared at me. I turned off my light. We sat in the dark. He took a breath and let his emotions seep through his clenched jaw. "I don't need your help."

I kept my hand on his arm for fear he'd lunge headfirst down the slope, oblivious to the danger, but also fearing I might miss out on something. He was strong, physically, but was obviously distraught and I was a little surprised when he spoke and made sense. A lot like I used to be—able to fool others into thinking I was smart, cool, logical during intense situations.

"Look … Mister—"

"Jeremy."

"Whatever. I made a big mistake. Kaylee needs me. It's awful and unfair. It was too destructive. But I have hope now."

"She's dying."

"Obviously," he responded. "But I brought her some new pills, and some vitamins, all bullshit, but I know that she needs to be here and I know I need to be with her."

"Okay," I said, "but –"

"But nothing," he responded, and stood, wobbly, almost falling.

I held him steady. "Let me help. What happens if you fall and hurt yourself? Then what? You'll be of no good to her then."

He stood trembling, waiting, as I quickly broke camp, stuffing my gear and tent haphazardly into my pack, and heaving it onto my shoulders, hoping that those Ambien crumbs amounted to nothing. I'd stayed awake on the stuff before and knew I wouldn't suddenly fall asleep—it was the delirium I worried about. Once, with a friend, I purposely took a lot, abusing it basically, just to see if I would learn anything.

We stood ready to descend, and Josh said, "I still resent you."

"What?"

"You've had a life. Why couldn't she?"

He leapt into the dark woods, and I followed, stumbling through the darkness, trying to stay steady. The sheer unfairness of it all had made me want to escape—Kaylee deserved so much more—and I wasn't able to deal with my level of empathy for her, rationalizing it all with a shrug, millions of people deserve better—so I had fled—just like Josh.

While trying to keep up with him, to "help" him, I tripped and nearly tumbled into a sharp branch from a fallen cracked tree blackened by lightning, and my ankles felt tight and swollen—my knees were fine—but there was an overall creakiness to my body in stark contrast to Josh, who was clearly not thinking about his body in the same way as I, as he flew downward, occasionally slowing, waiting for me to catch up—who was helping whom?

The slope flattened and Josh led me onto the footpath that he had apparently strayed from himself, and I followed easily now right behind him, pretty good I thought, considering, and I wondered as we approached the few lights in town left on—did he "resent" the others as well? Everyone was almost certainly older than Josh. Except the one teenage girl I'd seen on the first day who—where was she now? Had she preceded Kaylee? Was this town merely a place to die? Albeit with a much better view than most who were often stacked upon others half-dead in the high corridors of cities, people struggling to maintain what life they had left, fighting against all our transgressions. The night had descended into blackness with low looming clouds, what little light remaining reflecting on churning swirls and billowing tumbling lit gray black clouds.

I kept pace with Josh, stride for stride, shoulder to shoulder, as we arrived at what once was his house where he stayed with his wife Kaylee. He pushed the door open, slamming hard. Doctor Henry was in the dim-lit foyer, turning and facing us, perhaps only slightly surprised that we were not merely the wind.

Did Josh resent him?

He turned and led us back, not to the bedroom, but rather to a room seemingly attached just for this purpose: roof made of hard corrugated plastic, slanting like a hillbilly's shack, the floor slanting as well, strong, thick corner beams, one dim yellow light on the wall behind me, the back open to the night like an amphitheater, just enough room for spectator seats. In the middle, an oversized chair tilted slightly, resembling a flight seat ready for blast off, where Kaylee was wrapped in blankets and staring into the night.

Margery quietly rose from the seat next to her and offered it to Josh, who rushed forward, bumping into others, and embraced his wife and wept. Kaylee was calm, confident, magnanimous.

"You'll have a better life now," she said.

"No! Not without you."

Kaylee smiled. "You came back. You can live with yourself now."

Mentally, I distanced myself from this scene, dismissing it as a fabrication, as theater, telling myself that my taste of the Ambien powder colored my perception.

Josh buried his head into her chest and wept and a bolt of lightning lit the sky, the room, and everyone in it. He pulled out his packet of vitamins and miracle pills and pathetically tried to feed them to her while he mumbled about how it could help, about how he needed hope and the pills could help, and Kaylee pushed his arm away, pills dropping to the floor, and she seemed to have been holding on just long enough for him to come back to her.

When the dim yellow light suddenly went out, I was unnerved, and fought to remain detached while standing behind them all, searching for an escape route. The dark silhouettes, backs of nameless heads ... the lightning flashed, and I could just as easily have been in a horror film with aging movie stars. Where did I fit in? What was more frightening—the film or the old stars?

As the wind howled and rattled loose screws, and rain and hail came searing out of the heavens pounding the roof, we watched, and perhaps we collectively presumed that when the wind calmed for a moment, when the only sounds we could hear were Josh's choked sobs subsiding, in that moment, Kaylee passed, her spirit passing into another world, or as I mostly believed, her essence dissolving and reforming in the universe—

the slow decay of her parts—a process started long ago and not yet complete. That's how I constructed my thoughts, how I accepted the reality. Her last view of this earthly life was now immaterial, but what a spectacular view, a bizarre night landscape lit continuously by lightning accompanied by a symphony of thunder, rain, and hail.

As the storm subsided, and the yellow light blinked back on magically, the audience started rustling to their feet, and they seeped outside like rainwater, some passing me through the house, others out back directly into the rain-soaked night. I didn't know what to do. I stood against the wall, watching Margery lean over Kaylee and kiss her forehead while Josh buried his face into the blankets as if to breathe life back into her.

Doctor Henry appeared from nowhere and took Margery's hand and held it and I felt a totally irrational, yet gut-true jealousy. Why couldn't I hold her hand and why couldn't I feel her kiss—why did I want to connect with someone who took my heart leaping off a cliff with her? My jealously passed quickly as I thought it through, but also wondered about its power, rising up so suddenly without warning.

Doctor Henry mumbled something to her, probably the usual platitudes about better places, being at peace, seeing loved ones again, and all that claptrap. I didn't hear it—steeling myself against condolences as I usually did, as a mechanism for my own survival—what about George? His death did not seem nearly as ceremonious, nothing like all this. And where was Henry's wife Jackie? Her process seemed so unfair.

Gray dawn sky cracked the storm and Josh completed whatever mental process or ritual he was going through. No way of knowing for sure because our actions told so little of the story. One could only assume that he was remembering, maybe visualizing times he'd had with Kaylee, arguments maybe, but mostly the good stuff, the first meeting, adventures together leading up to their wedding; a common scenario, and perhaps this moment for Josh was emblematic of all human suffering. Maybe his feelings were so essential that we all share them intimately. Empathy for him was unavoidable and made me feel miserable—I could only guess what he was thinking based on my own experiences, and since I was apparently "just like Josh," maybe I should have understood more. But I didn't understand. Obviously his thoughts were deeply personal. But were they unique? Should I ask, like some ambitious news reporter, *hey Josh hey, how do you feel right now?* Could he even begin to adequately describe and relate his thoughts and feelings? Hell, I could barely discern my own—such were my thoughts at that moment.

Thankfully, Josh didn't prolong our agony. He stood and, while passing me, shoved what was left of his little bag of miracle pills into my hand, then hugged Margery and made his way through the house, out the front door into the gray dawn, and disappeared back into the forest, presumably never to be seen by me or the others here or anywhere again.

Doctor Henry had already left without me noticing—must've slipped out with the others. I'd assumed he would do something with Kaylee's body, but then I could almost hear his voice—*I'm not a mortician.* And I wondered if someone in the town was—clearly there was a need for one.

Margery glanced at the doorway as if trying to decide how to get away from me, and I felt a pressing need to explain why I left her and Kaylee when they needed me most. Then again, that seemed an arrogant presumption—they didn't need me at all. But if Margery didn't need me—did she, or could she, at least want me? And if so, what should I say to her? The only thing I could think of at that moment was full of inadequate practicality and misplaced accusation.

"What is this?" I asked, and held the bag in front of her. The room had filled with gray light.

"Desperation," Margery said.

"Yeah," I responded, "I get that, but did it have any chance of helping her?"

In that pallid light, Margery looked tired and probably was, although I could never be sure, as she always seemed precariously balanced between healthy exhilaration and resignation.

"I don't know," she said. "Maybe, and maybe tumors melt away in the light of pure belief. What do you think?"

I'd often thought about belief affecting reality, thinking about it relentlessly off and on over many years, and I dismissed it now as I had done in the past, with my usual frustration. "Anything's possible."

Margery smiled wanly, "Then it's possible for you to love me, isn't it?"

What the fuck did that mean? And why was I suddenly pissed off? I thought I had successfully detached myself from my raw attraction to her, at least enough to think rationally and not obsess on her words like some insecure little boy. Instead, I was thinking she had to know I'd been taken by her from the start, and that she had toyed with my heart mercilessly, tossing it from the cliff with each death-defying leap. Or maybe that was going too far—maybe she'd done very little that she wouldn't have done anyway.

"Anything," I repeated, "is possible."

The overcast light was filling the room, and only a few paces away Kaylee, or Kaylee's body, was stiffening, facing what might have been her last view had she hung on for another hour or so, an ethereal mist threading through a meadow full of wildflowers, wet petals glistening and sparkling in rays of sunlight tentatively trying to peek through the shroud. For a moment, I felt at peace.

A ray of sunlight burst forth in a hopelessly magical and timeless moment, the beam focused—directly illuminating Doctor Henry's wife Jackie standing in the meadow naked, her aged body drooping as if she wore wet clothes, her skin folding and white-wet, waterlogged yet dazzling in the sun.

The ubiquitous group of hikers paused on their trail and watched. From the other side of the meadow, Doctor Henry was striding briskly through tall grass and wildflowers toward her, the green light of her ankle bracelet holding steady. Margery rushed out the back and I followed her.

We all began to converge on Jackie standing insane in the middle of the meadow with the forest and cliff rising behind her, and I felt a little like a cowboy trying to capture a wild horse, only this mare was in her death throes and her wildness was fueled by an ephemeral mind-body spirit, the mind and body connected in a grand gesture, ready for a grand transition, in a place where death seemed common, yet couched in "healthy living"—I was one with my trail mix, one with my granola, one with my gorp, and God and nature, and the flight of my spirit escaping into the forest until one day I would make my inevitable ultimate escape.

Doctor Henry stepped carefully toward his wife, and Jackie tilted her head back, long white hair lifted by the mist and fog as the sunlight struggled through the grayness.

"Jackie!" Doctor Henry yelled.

"No!" she screamed. "No!" Then she settled into an incoherent mumble.

Doctor Henry moved closer, startling her. She turned toward the hikers and cringed, her body moving on instinct. What was left of it; likely she would collapse at any moment, her brain forgetting how to stand, how to put one step in front of another, forgetting soon how to take her next breath. She looked at me. She smiled. *Weird,* I thought. *What does that mean?* Then she pivoted and stumbled toward the rising forest and cliff and stream.

"Jackie," Doctor Henry said. "One last kiss?"

She paused and Doctor Henry moved closer, slowly, finally coming upon her, careful not to startle her, touching her arm, leaning close and touching her lips with his, searching her half-shut eyes for life. Jackie had not responded to his kiss. He tried again to no response, and then one more time, and Jackie kissed him as if they were young lovers, a first and last kiss disappearing in the mist rising from a meadow full of wildflowers, and then Jackie forgot how to breathe and collapsed, leaving Doctor Henry kneeling over her body crumpled amid the brilliant blue wildflowers, and yellow, red, orange flowers spreading from the blue core, and the full sun bursting forth miraculously from the gray morning and lighting us all.

10

MAYBE WE WERE ALL JUST "STONED," high on cannabis, but it was a sight—one that I obviously haven't forgotten.

The hikers closed in and we formed a circle around Jackie's body in the bed of wildflowers, the blue and red-orange hue, like the flowers were growing through her. Now we had two bodies. What were we going to do with them? Surely not a shallow grave like George must have wanted. Proper grave digging in this terrain would take lots of work—cremation might be a good idea.

Henry removed her green light ankle-bracelet and directed us, Margery and I joining the others in lifting Jackie's body, carrying it like pallbearers—obviously no casket—and the body with no clothes, loose skin providing handles, the skin preparing to melt back into the earth. We carried her, following Doctor Henry on a path through the forest on the south end of town where the two streams met, flowing down river through the gorge and into the valley—and where there was constructed, far in advance, a funeral pyre, and I laughed—*what else?* I thought—*why not?* I thought—*and what the hell am I doing here?* I thought, overcome with anxiety. Who would be next? Would I eventually end atop a bonfire?

Following Doctor Henry's instructions, we climbed logs strategically placed for us to lay Jackie flat on her back staring up into what was now a bright, blue-lit cloudless sky. Doctor Henry shouted at us to make sure her eyes were open—the way she wanted it, he said. I found it hard to imagine a scene in which Jackie told him to keep her eyes open while reclining atop a funeral pyre.

Somehow, by luck, good or bad, I had positioned myself near her face, balancing on the pyre across from a solemn-looking hiker who seemed inordinately calm. He nodded at the eyes, half shut, as if expecting me to do something, pry them open I suspected, so I touched her cool eyelids and pushed them up as far as I could, even though the lids immediately started to droop back to their original half-shut position. We clambered down the pyre and stood with Henry as he said a few words—well-worn and meaningless—or perhaps comforting in their familiarity and full of meaning for this type of moment—words designated by the Almighty. I didn't listen much.

Margery had drifted to the other side of the group—or I'd stumbled down the wrong side—either way, she wasn't with me, and I wondered how Henry might set this pile of rain-soaked wood on fire. I envisioned torches of some sort but then my thoughts wandered into the practicality of torches and their fantastical depictions, especially in fiction, and film, and loosely-told factual reporting.

Doctor Henry stooped behind a rock at the base of the pyre, lifted a bright red, plastic gasoline container and emptied it, splashing it everywhere, the air itself filling with gas, then he took out a pink Bic lighter. Concentrating on his stiff thumb, he struggled getting it to ignite. A surprisingly robust whoosh of flames engulfed him and then sucked forward into the core of the pyre, the wood crackling quickly ablaze, flames leaping high around Jackie's body and lapping at the blue sky. And the stench of her burning flesh drifted in the breeze, the smoke like a campfire after someone had tossed in a Styrofoam plate.

The sun had risen and now beat down with mid-morning heat, helping the fire do its job while I kept glancing at the others looking for some direction, especially at Doctor Henry, who managed to conduct this ritual with little deference to religion—other than a sort of cover-all-your-bases approach—not much of ritualistic traditions—except maybe the funeral pyre.

The hikers abruptly reformed into their group, as if someone had flipped a switch or an allotted time had passed, or someone had just finished removing a rock from their shoe, and they murmured and joked and resumed their trek into the forest, later than intended but with their usual enthusiasm.

What about Kaylee? Would we burn her as well? Where was her funeral pyre? Or would we cook her in the coals smoldering in the pile of Jackie's ashes?

Margery looked at me and turned away, heading back up the trail, through the trees, to the now-washed-out bright meadow of wildflowers, and my tooth chose that moment to begin throbbing, an excruciating, intense pain radiating through my skull that made me buckle over and hold my jaw, as if that would do any good.

I stumbled toward Doctor Henry, his eyes still fixated on the remaining fire, and fell in front of him, on my knees like a beggar—funny how all else fades into insignificance when experiencing intense pain, no matter how seemingly ridiculous the source. Nothing in the world mattered except ridding myself of physical pain. I was intensely focused on my back left molar, and all my previous tormenting thoughts shrank to insignificance—in that way, I welcomed the pain. I embraced it, the agony was good. Was I Catholic? Conversely, I believed that if it weren't for the pain I would be able to endure all the emotional onslaughts—if the pain would just go away, I would be able to handle everything just fine.

"Doctor," I said, "help me."

With one hand on my jaw, I reached toward him. He looked down at me, and spoke flatly, emotionless. "What's the trouble?"

"My tooth."

He felt my neck, a move doctors instinctively made, apparently from the instant they escaped their mother's womb. "Hmm," he said. "Open."

I opened my mouth and without any prompting said, "Ah." The wind shifted and I inhaled funeral smoke and coughed and sputtered.

"Hmm," he said again. "Looks like you might have an abscess, which could lead to septicemia, which could lead to sepsis, which could cut off oxygen to your vital organs, including your brain … you could have about a month left."

Margery

I struggled to my feet. "What the hell are you talking about? I have a broken molar."

"George is the dentist."

"He's dead." Which was painfully obvious of course, but saying it out loud somehow deflected my tooth agony. The pain radiating and throbbing through my skull subsided just enough for me to conclude my head hurt because I was stressed out, and such pain only occurred as essential panic; that is, when I couldn't emotionally understand a situation.

"See me this afternoon," the doctor said, "and I'll see what I can do."

"Should it be removed … extracted?"

"Don't know—I'm not a dentist."

Henry stepped around me and resumed his selfish fixation on his wife's fire, and I felt guilty for interrupting him. And suddenly, as if he had taken a stick and stabbed it into the back of my head, the searing pain returned worse than ever, accompanied by a curious terror—maybe I had a brain tumor, maybe like Kaylee. Or George.

I headed along the trail, through the trees, the unrelenting pain and irrational fear fueling my movement—move fast or it will kill you—and I marched on, intent on finding Margery. I rationalized my headache as merely a side effect from my tooth combined with the intense sun—nothing to worry about—it would all go away once I found Margery—where was she? Was she now my only salvation? But no single person could be anyone's salvation. Margery obviously had her own troubles. Still, I wanted to hold her, believing that in her arms I would find peace and my pain would disappear.

Craving normalcy, or at least the impression of normalcy, I walked up the road to her house, wanting merely to call upon her on this fine sunny day as if I were one of those happy hikers stopping in to say hello and have a pleasant chat, talk about the weather, the continuing erosion of the roads and the need for maintenance, and what might be for dinner.

While calling her name, I went inside as if I owned the place, and searched through the rooms, but there was no sign of her anywhere. I hiked to the meadow behind Kaylee's house, and stood in the bright sunlight, baking in the midday heat, peering like a peeping tom into the death porch, Kaylee presumably looking back at me from her space seat, her cockpit taking her to the stars and beyond. I felt like a spaceman, a lost crew member from Kaylee's ship, left behind on an awfully strange planet. Where was Margery? Had she also been abandoned?

I hoisted myself onto the corner of the porch, one foot dangling over a wilting red flower, Kaylee still there in her space chair, facing me, staring at me, but no sign of Margery. Where the hell was she … was she, I thought, wondering if the echo of my thoughts came from a serious health condition. Who was going to dispose of Kaylee's body if not Margery? I called for her again and again to no response.

What was I doing—they weren't my concern. Why was I trying to bury Kaylee? Ridiculous, I thought. Stop this nonsense. Where were my things? Where had I left my backpack?

I circled around the house, vaguely aware I'd dropped my pack near the front door the night before when I had arrived with Josh. Was I ready, again, to leave? Like Josh. To disappear from this landscape, escape back to a life at least more predictable in its march toward the same end. Was it the same? Was there any way to make it predictable, "normal," easy? Did what lay on the other side of the ridge constitute a more sane life, and end, than where I was now?

I hugged my backpack while lying on the front steps leading to Kaylee's porch and waited. For what, I don't know. If I did nothing, of course, that was something, so I waited for something to happen.

Then it occurred to me that Margery might at that moment be on the edge of her cliff ready to make another death-defying leap, but was fairly sure the timing wasn't right, based on no other reason than intuition. So I waited, and inevitably doubt crept in.

Should I climb up there to look for her? Even if she was there, what good would it do for me to watch her? She would just jump again, without me. Damn, I was in a pickle—that's what trying to phrase my situation in logical terms produced—thoughts about pickles, and then visions of dill pickles dancing around in my head.

Inaction only made my tooth throb more, and before I could even think about climbing back up to the top of that damn cliff to search for Margery, I had to go to the dentist … or in this case to my afternoon doctor "appointment" with Doctor Henry. Was it a choice?

I heaved on my pack, for no particular reason except that it was part of me, and I had no home without it and did not want to leave it

Margery

unattended again. I suppose, in lieu of anything else, it centered me. It also felt heavy, and it occurred to me that I hadn't slept at all.

After the appointment, maybe I would ask the doctor about Kaylee's body and then I would play it cool and inquire about Margery, maybe find out something about her because really I knew very little—nothing. Who was she? Did it matter? Was her past relevant to the now? Was mine? What of the future? What if her bungee cord finally broke? Why was I afraid of "losing" Margery, a person I'd only recently met and could lay no reasonable claim to? She wasn't "mine" in any sense of the word. Nobody ever really possessed another person—sometimes, if we are very lucky, we momentarily share the same space and time as one. I had not yet had that with her but knew it was entirely possible. What I might "lose" was the possibility of her touch—not enough, I reasoned, not enough to override my tooth pain. Besides, no way was she diving to her death just yet, and so my trip to Doctor Henry was the most reasonable course.

No one else was around as I hiked up the road to his house—not that there were many to begin with and I'd met almost all of them at least once and still couldn't remember any names. One person trudged by, probably late for his morning jog, but I couldn't really know for sure if he was late, early, or on time, as I knew nothing about him. He was just the guy in sweats, looking as if he were trying desperately to get in shape.

Doctor Henry seemed surprised to see me lugging my backpack toward him as he stood outside holding a glass of water, sipping it, and contemplating something unfathomable—at least that's how I interpreted his brow furrowing at the same time he gazed blankly toward the forest. Without looking at me, he asked, "You headed somewhere?"

"To see you."

"Is it time?"

The sun was almost straight overhead, soon to arc toward the cliff. "I believe so."

He looked up. "Close enough."

I set my pack down and followed him into the kitchen, expecting him to lead me back to the cocktail party room where he had fed Kaylee her psilocybin, but he told me to sit at the kitchen table and lean my head back. Then he rattled around in a drawer and pulled out a flashlight.

"You are a doctor, aren't you? I mean, an MD, and not just a Ph.D?"

"Of course ... why?"

"Shouldn't you be using your professional equipment?"

"My scope is recharging. This will work just fine."

It was an industrial-sized flashlight with duct tape on the handle, presumably holding in the batteries, but at least the beam was bright as he flashed it into my eyes while putting on a pair of glasses, and then he peered into my mouth and hummed his doctor mantra, "Hmm. Ah. Hmm," then told me to close my mouth. He stared me straight in the eyes, and began a somewhat disjointed diagnosis, the most I'd heard him say at one time. "The molar ... forgot what number it is ... it's in pretty bad shape. Not sure you could do a root canal. My guess is that it should be extracted. But you don't want me doing it –"

"Right," I interrupted, "because you're not George."

"I could try taking it out but there really is no reason to right now. As far as I can tell, there's no infection ... at least not a serious one. There might be some debris in the gums, but I can't see it. You might have had nerve damage, but the nerves must be dead by now, otherwise you'd be screaming bloody murder. So why risk an extraction? You're fine." His words were more or less reassuring, but then he took off his glasses and added, "Of course it could always be something else."

Something else? Panic rose to my chest as I stared at him, his gray hair, eyes now seeming a little murky and I wondered if he could see at all—had he missed something important? Because, after all, he might have been a little distracted by his wife dying. Shouldn't I at least say something—what had happened to my propensity for too much empathy? Was I only empathetic when feeling energetic? Did sick people suck the life out of us until we became sick as well? I had been bracing myself against feeling too much, and now I felt like a coward.

"Sorry," I said, "for your loss."

Saying those words almost always felt fake, and the words often were, but this time I meant it—deeply sincere—feeling his loss enveloping me in despair. Doctor Henry didn't bother responding. He grimaced; likely the process of giving me a diagnosis had taken his mind off his own pain, and I felt inadequate to the task of helping him heal. I thanked him, filled my water bottle, went outside, and hoisted my pack again, and walked down the road. The afternoon sun was at its most intense, angling from the west, extraordinarily hot, and sweat trickled down my back.

Only when I stood alone in the seemingly deserted town did I think again about Kaylee's body. I had "forgotten" to ask him about that. What was there for me to do? Kaylee was not my problem. None of these people were. I had no history with them aside from the past several days ... of which I'd lost count, because I hadn't slept last night or all the way through soundly any night since I'd been here, and I thought about emptying my pack in the dirt, searching for an Ambien that wasn't there.

I looked back at Henry's house, the dining room with its nineteenth century décor, and the notable absence of photos—no mementos or pictures or much of anything that indicated any of these people had much of a past here any more than I did. They occupied homes as if they were only passing through—were they all merely vacationers, rich people who owned this basin high in the mountains away from the strain of everyday life below? I suppose that was possible, although I hadn't seen anyone pack up their things and climb into one of those old trucks parked forever near the one road leading high along the gorge pass and down into the valley.

I gazed up at the eastern ridge and calculated, by the angle of the hot afternoon sun, I could be on the back side of the ridge before sunset and possibly camp near the spot where I'd met Josh and Kaylee. If I started, just took one step in that direction, I could build up my momentum again and might make it. All it took was resolve—and I would be gone.

But, of course, there was one thing keeping me from taking that step.

11

WHERE WAS SHE? I'd seen her each of the few days I'd been here, so where was she now, on this starkly bright and oddly bleak cloudless day? A day for swimming or sitting in the shade with a cold beer, a day for avoiding the blistering sun.

My stomach gurgled and turned, cramped and subsided, and I considered going back to the doctor and asking for food, a snack or something, but conversation would be time-consuming and I couldn't wait a moment longer. I rummaged through my backpack, dirty clothes falling onto the ground, eventually finding a small daypack that I'd shoved in at the last minute, just in case I wanted to set up a base camp and explore, or just in case I needed to climb to the top of a cliff and find a puzzling woman.

Half of an old protein bar was flattened and stuck to the bottom of the day pack—left over from a previous trip. I peeled the wrapper off in pieces, stuck the grimy synthetic food into my mouth, and chewed on my good side, dirt and rocks crunching like broken bits of my tooth. It felt and tasted like a bicycle tire—not that I've ever eaten one. I rolled up an extra shirt, my bottle of water, and the last of my crumbled-up nuts and stuffed it all into my daypack.

Margery

I left my backpack unattended again, this time in some brush next to an abandoned house, and headed toward the cliff, pausing at Margery's house, deciding to go in, and shouting her name to no response, opening all doors and finding nothing, realizing that I could have looked for food there and stolen some only after leaping across the white water gushing between the boulders, and struggling up the talus slope, washed out and colorless in the hot sun, sweat on my brow, stinging my eyes, sliding on the loose rock, ankles bleeding from a tumbling rat-sized rock, slowing, remembering my caution the other times taking this route, and on up quickly to the top where I found … nothing. Not a damn thing, no nylon webbing wrapped around trees, no bungee cord coiled like a snake, no cord sloping over the edge—nothing. *What the fuck,* I thought—eloquently of course.

"Margery."

The air was dead, trees still, sun stuck in the sky like it was three o'clock in the afternoon for the rest of my life.

Then it wasn't. Then it was ten minutes or so later, and a shadow had appeared on the flat edge from somewhere.

"Margery!" I called and the shadow, upon close examination, was from a tree branch, as if trees moved like humans. Maybe they did, but more likely it was a function of the rotation of the earth and the angle of sunlight and my sleep-deprived addled mind becoming prone to hallucinations in the heat. I felt positively on edge—literally and figuratively. Maybe it was a religious experience.

I stepped closer to the rim of the cliff, took off my day pack, and drank water, wondering if hydration was the key to sanity. I gasped for air and sipped and did it again, then stupidly poured water on my head and peered over the edge, for the first time seriously studying the trajectory of the leap. *If I dare,* I thought, *yes, I could swan-dive off and swoosh into the water, immerse myself in the cold clear stream, a hydration of the soul, an immersion in God's holy water, a baptism of sorts,* something that at that moment made absolutely perfect sense; that is, until I considered the depth of the stream below.

I could see flashes of water downstream through the tops of trees, and then disappearing into the forest—and unless the laws of physics had changed, the stream continued, perpetually merging with the other stream at the confluence before it crashed down the gorge into the long valley and was sucked up by the cities beyond.

I had a clear shot, a straight, gravity-induced path to the inviting water—Margery had known what she was doing, playing with the danger, perhaps hoping that the cord would break, or even counting on it—surely she had a backup plan. Looking down, I felt every molecule in my body pulling me over the edge—we are, after all, mostly water and water runs downhill, waterfalls never fall up, except as mist, so nothing too strange about my body flowing over the edge like water—nothing to do with suicidal tendencies or anything—no, I'd never attempted suicide, at least not blatantly—in that way, I thought, I was normal. *But what about Margery? And where was she?*

"I'm right here," she said.

Although I have experienced auditory hallucinations over my lifetime (at least in the general sense, thinking I'd heard something or someone when I didn't), I was pretty sure this was real.

I whirled around and nearly passed out, dizzy, short choppy breaths, the gravity behind me tugging as I wobbled, before lurching forward and shaking some clarity into my head, looking at her, drawn to her as powerfully as I was drawn to the water below—Margery altering the universe enough to bring me back from the edge.

I caught my breath, and tried to see her as if for the first time—maybe I had missed something revealing in her outward appearance—she was slender, almost skinny, and she had a distinct nose and face, worn, sharply accentuated, bony; her eyes maintained a natural reflection, mirroring the surroundings, the environment. And, in my looking, in my inept search for who she was, I detected something fading—not in my attraction to her, that was as strong as ever. But in her … what? Essence, her energy? The physiological cloud of bacteria and humanness that surrounds us all? An aura?

Normally, or at least in the past few days of so-called normalcy, she abounded with energy—now, however, maybe because of the afternoon heat and the unusual lack of a breeze, she seemed to be wilting. Even so, I wanted nothing more than to lay down with her in my arms and share a dream world together—knowing of course that our actual dreams would be separate—but being in a dream together, inhabiting the same dream, was so appealing I couldn't easily let go of the idea.

Margery

Margery stood next to a stunted tree—her bungee equipment concealed behind untethered bare legs, and she stepped toward me, or at least so I thought. She stared at the ground, at the rock, the small crags and pools of stagnant rain water, discolored by the organic material seeping into it, and she made a move as if she were passing a stranger on a crowded city street.

I blocked her way, and she looked up—we stared at each other—her touch so close yet so elusive. I wanted her in my arms, but her stance, her look, all betrayed an effort to avoid me, a magnet on the negative side, pushing me away. Out of the corners of her eyes, perhaps from the heat, tears appeared—as if by magic—silent, tiny streams making their way down the craggy landscape of her face, crow's feet diverting them, small pools gathering on the ridge of her upper lips, mixing with sweat, and I longed for the salty taste of her lips touching mine. Then the flow dried up. She set her jaw, determined to show self-control, exhibiting a steel will that only increased my admiration for her.

"Please," she said, "get out of my way."

"Why?"

In hindsight, it was a selfish, almost cowardly question. I didn't want to take responsibility, and I was indecisive. I should have grabbed her, at that moment or sooner, but I didn't know how she might respond—would my forceful attempt merely stiffen her resistance? Or would it allow her to merge into my arms? Did it matter? I couldn't stand it anymore—my heart soaring and sinking with her every movement, her every breath, and when she made a feint left, I leaned with her. She sprinted right, and I nearly fell.

She ran—running just as before when attached to her cord—but this time she ran unbound, free, and she hurled herself over the edge flying—a spirit—floating, hanging in mid-air, forever, arms and legs caressing tranquil air—then vanishing as if she never existed.

The air pulled from my lungs arced over the edge forever attached to her, choking and wheezing *No,* inhaling and coughing, sucking in a full breath and screaming, "No!"

Standing a safe distance away, hands trembling, I wondered if yelling "No" had repudiated my feelings for her—allowing me to sever myself from Margery, terrified of following her and throwing myself into the void, and why should I? Maybe she wanted to kill herself, but why should I?

After a while, I don't know how long, the far ridge was gaining its late afternoon brightness and glow, and the shadows had overtaken me. I inched toward the edge and tentatively peered over—but no sign of her, only what I'd seen before—the clear water directly below disappearing into the forest downstream—perhaps where Margery had gone. I knelt in the shadow and felt a sudden evening updraft, a breeze—maybe Margery was just waiting for the right conditions to make her most daring jump, maybe she had measured the depth of the water, the angle of her trajectory effected by the wind, and had waited for a windless day, her leap measured to perfection, and therefore maybe she was alive—waiting for me—but that hope quickly gave way to despair and I lay on my stomach, arms outstretched over the void, my shirt dampened by one of the dirty rainwater pools, and I wept—I sobbed uncontrollably, inconsolable, unable to stop, my tears a waterfall joining Margery in her leap and I was in a timeless state—a perpetual mourning from which I'd never escape—except for the slow, yet fast, encroachment of the evening and a stronger breeze wafting up from the stream below like Margery's phantom kisses, and I rolled over onto my back and stared up at a hint of a star or hallucination, leaving me nothing but searing curiosity, a compulsion to know why. Why hadn't Margery and I ever kissed, why hadn't we held onto one another, shared an evening, and how could I have felt such a deep spiritual and physical connection to her?

As the sun blazed on the far ridge—blood red—I knelt, suppressed an urge to beg for a miracle, then stood and gathered my small day pack, finishing my water, and eating my nuts. I smiled. Nuts. Maybe Margery was a little crazy. I often sensed a whimsical humor waiting to be released, or rediscovered in her. Maybe she was dangerously insane—but if so, what did that make me? Just some guy sitting on the edge of a cliff eating his nuts?

I packed away my food and empty water bottle, then bravely looked over the edge again. And gravity once again lured me, enticed me, begged me to jump. I imagined Margery below waving me on. I could, I thought, but in a way she'd given me a reason not to, a purpose—she had told me nothing, had been cryptic, and by doing so she had ripped away my veneer and left me confronting my natural human impulse for discovery.

I was alone, but I was used to being alone. More importantly, I was alive, almost reborn, possessed with a driving curiosity, a fierce will to understand why this had happened. Why had she jumped? I could choose to hurl myself off the cliff or could continue my quest to understand her and to understand how I felt about her. I turned away and began my chaotic descent, dislodging rocks, grabbing onto branches, sliding down the steep slope in the rapidly diminishing light.

I looked for her, or for her body, as one might look for a lost wallet or car keys, searching for a long time before giving up. That's normal, isn't it? Doesn't mean we objectify our loved ones, does it?

I don't know. I only knew that Margery felt as if she were still with me and now her touch would be forever out of reach, like Keats' Grecian urn or Gatsby's green light. Maybe literary allusions were good for something, but I drew upon my protective sense of reality—some might say cynicism—and recalled pessimistic euphemisms about being careful about what you wish for. What if Margery and I had experienced love—would the natural progression of our relationship have taken us to the usual familiarity, comfort, and eventual irritations and bickering? Or were Margery and I too wise for that sort of thing? Did love at our age help negate the mistakes of youth?

While worthy questions, those weren't the ones that would help ease my pain—I needed more immediate answers. Why would Margery throw herself off a cliff? If she had "loved" me as Kaylee said, why couldn't she tell me herself? Why didn't she allow our love to flourish? I had never actually used the word "love" when I spoke with her, had I? Never said, *Margery, I love you.*

I stood next to the stream in deep shadow, staring at the cliff and looking for a bungee cord to magically appear so I could revise the truth, and searched downstream along the footpath she must've taken often in her return, and then searched further along the shoreline where the brush showed signs of having been trampled upon—presumably by George the dentist, and I remembered that my tooth didn't hurt at all—until now when I thought about it—and then thought about the doctor, Doctor Henry, and his equivocal "diagnosis" and my head hurt but it led me to turn around—back to him—maybe he had the answers—at the very least, someone needed to be told about Margery ... I searched the stream, now black in the shadows and the looming night, and then crashed through the brush, headed back to Doctor Henry.

Nearing my backpack, I looked at Kaylee's house and wondered if her body was decaying, and wondered what the process was like—could you see decay—when did it start to smell bad, how soon? Tempted to look, I marched on, exhausted and hungry—all I had eaten was that hard, plaque-like chunk of protein bar and a handful of nuts. And I hadn't slept—I folded my daypack and shoved it deep into the womb of my backpack—the weight of my pack and of the events bore down on me as I struggled, one step in front of the other, more difficult than any of my mountain climbs. My lips felt dry and cracked and mouth parched—I'd spent the day in a furnace, my stomach cramped, my face felt like there was a permanent layer of dirt on it, and I coughed, sending a searing pain up the back of my neck, exploding from the top of my head.

Doctor Henry's house was dark, no light, nothing, and I felt my heart sink—how would I get answers from the blackness?—but I struggled on, up his front steps, and banged on the door, once, twice, and tried calling out but my throat felt constricted and the blackness engulfed me, pushing me to my knees, where I began muttering Margery's name. While I don't remember any of it, this is the state Doctor Henry said he found me in, on my knees, and weeping—similar to my embarrassment at his wife's funeral pyre—how insignificant my tooth pain seemed in comparison—now my sobs stemmed from a loss remotely resembling his—mourning for someone else and not myself—but really, is there much difference between the two?

12

WHEN I WOKE, daylight was surrounding me—bright and cheerful. I was lying on the same table-bed that Kaylee had her psilocybin trip treatment, an IV in my arm. Few people go through their lives without at least once having an IV, so I wasn't too startled by it, but did wonder what the crazy Doctor Henry put in that clear plastic bag.

"Just fluids," he said, stepping next to me.

"How'd you know?"

"Know what?"

"What I was thinking."

"I logically assumed that you were wondering what was in the bag," he said, "and I was correct, wasn't I?"

"Apparently."

"You were dehydrated." He disconnected the IV and was peeling tape from my arm, ripping out hair, stinging like bees.

If I'd been that dehydrated, then maybe my entire encounter with Margery had been one big dehydration-induced hallucination … but the hopeful moment, I calculated, lasted less than a millisecond. I knew the current reality all too well.

Margery

Doctor Henry removed the needle, a spot of blood oozing out as he told me to hold down the cotton ball. I sat up and felt woozy, hungry, but otherwise "normal."

Doctor Henry invited me outside on the deck, where not too long ago, Margery and I stood together staring at her cliff, standing so close and so connected, yet without touching. He offered me watermelon—the best for recovering from dehydration—and toast, and it sparked my hunger, and he fed me oatmeal with blueberries, just as she had done, and I began to feel whole again, the food abating my hunger, and my longing for Margery, a little—I felt calm and wondered if hunger could have accounted for my desire. But that logic worked for only a few moments, replaced by the desire to share blueberries with her—enjoy the peaceful, satisfied smile playing across her face and the fantasy that we could smile together forever, kissing and wiping the oatmeal from our lips, our attraction building through the day, culminating into a heavenly passion as the evening stars appeared and again before we fell asleep side by side dreaming.

I tortured myself with such thoughts while sipping coffee and staring at Doctor Henry, his gray hair, his weathered face and bony hands, as he sat silently finishing his breakfast, and I waited, annoyed by his silence. If he could read my thoughts, why didn't he start answering my questions?

"I don't understand any of this. What's going on?"

Doctor Henry turned to me and smiled grimly, paternally. "Be more specific."

Where would I start? Doctor Henry was staring at me now, impatient, a look I'd given many people before; those people getting younger and younger—a joke of course, but one that gained more teeth the older I got. Doctor Henry was older than I—no question about that. So, with my hunger and thirst sated, I approached it all a bit more methodically, and I hoped rationally.

"Your wife, I'm sorry ... you don't have to tell me, but she was suffering from Alzheimer's?"

"It was a blessing she died when she did, such a beautiful place ... it was advanced dementia, not quite the same, but close enough."

"And ..." I forged on, "Kaylee?"

"Brain tumor ... like the dentist."

I wondered if that explained George's happiness, abnormal pressure on his brain, and waited for more explanation from the doctor.

"Didn't know him well," he said. "Never really got along with him ..."

While still curious about George ... there were more pressing matters. "And what of Kaylee's body?"

Doctor Henry shook his head, grimaced, and rubbed his hands through his unkempt white hair. "Josh left, so someone has to take care of her ... there really is no organization or protocol. Things just happen or they don't."

"But you—"

"I'm not in charge."

I stared at him, a man tired of being responsible for others. "The psilocybin treatment?" I asked. "Obviously that didn't work."

Doctor Henry snapped back. "Of course it worked. What the hell are you talking about? Oh, I get it, you think that it was supposed to cure her, to give her a long wonderful life of hallucinogenic bliss. Maybe immortality? Is that what you were thinking? We're all here in this paradise-like town because we're chasing immortality? Well, obviously that's not the case, is it?"

I waited. Maybe he'd always been cantankerous, but this was the first I'd seen of it.

"The treatment worked," he said. "Kaylee was terrified. She was suffering mental distress. After the treatment, she was ... accepting, aware, ready for passage, I don't know, but I do know that for those last hours of her life, she was happy. I only wish we had done it sooner. Maybe she would have had a better time with Josh. Who the fuck knows."

The paternal Doctor Henry seemed to have vanished. He slurped his coffee and fumed as the sun rose to mid-morning, and I worried my approach was all wrong, asking about Margery last, but how could I hold back now?

"Again, Doctor Henry, sorry for ... everything really ..."

He waved his hand. "Not your fault ... call me Henry."

But weren't we all guilty? My mere presence made me a conspirator of some sort, didn't it? Regardless of how I felt, I needed to press on. "What about Margery?"

Margery

He looked at me, clearly calculating what to say or not say. "What about her?"

I opened my mouth to answer but couldn't make a sound, my thoughts jumbled into incomprehension, and felt a profound inability to express myself, to even put together a question, drowning in ordinary yet inexplicable feelings. I took a deep breath and tried to organize and measure out specific questions, and ended up blurting, "I love her!"

I felt like a fool, and it didn't help when Doctor Henry burst out laughing—*Ha. Ha. Ha. Ha.* Tears seeped from his eyes as he heaved with his breathtaking, hearty laughter.

What the hell kind of response was that? The more he tried to recover from his laughing, the angrier I became.

"Stop!" I yelled, and felt like a toddler struggling to make sense of the world.

He breathed normally and looked at me. I sensed pity, and that pissed me off even more, but contained myself.

He stood, picked up the breakfast plates, started back to the kitchen, stopped, and said, "More coffee?"

Screw the coffee, I thought, but managed to be polite about it. "No," I said, "no thank you."

He paused. "Let's go check on Kaylee—I'll try to answer your questions as best I can after we take care of her."

Seeing Kaylee's body did not sound like much fun, but whatever motives or emotions Doctor Henry had toward me or anyone else, clearly he knew a lot more about Margery than I did, so if I was going to learn anything, I would have to follow him and listen, allow him to give me directions like he'd done at the fire. We walked down the road in mid-morning sunlight, the day cooler, like other normal days leading to the end of a season—further proving yesterday unusual.

A few people magically appeared alongside us, and I recognized them from Kaylee's trip-treatment and cocktail party. But things don't happen by magic, they only appear to, and this Kaylee group must have been prearranged, at least loosely, within the parameters of this town. All I knew was I did not want to touch death, especially in the intimate way I had at the funeral pyre, so this time I would hide behind Doctor

Henry, ready to trail away into the woods and reemerge only when absolutely necessary.

Others lifted Kaylee onto their shoulders, her stiff statue-body positioned as if she were still sitting in her spaceship seat forever poised to view the lightning. Her eyes seemed shut, peacefully sleeping, although it could have been a corpse's ruse, eyes open just a slit, just enough to catch a glimpse of the meadow where she was about to be buried.

Enough of death. I choose life! That's what I was telling myself, selling it hard, as they dug a grave in the meadow. I occupied my thoughts by trying to figure out why the Kaylee group was able to dig deep into rocky, rich meadow soil while George's grave near the stream bank was nearly impenetrable, and settled upon a plausible answer—the stream water washed away topsoil leaving solid rock.

They positioned Kaylee in her grave as if she might want to blast off and explore distant galaxies—maybe she was already there. Then they started shoveling dirt into her face, and once covered, they repositioned as best they could the dislodged clumps of wildflowers. Were others buried here?

I eased away, standing next to a tall, blue wildflower moving gently in the breeze and skeptically waited for someone to make an inept comparison between Kaylee and the flowers, some inevitable, inadequate verse that would float away in the wind and do nothing to relieve the suffering of those still living. My cynicism was threatening to spiral into more suffering, so I decided to talk my way out of the vortex.

While we were all standing in what felt like arbitrary silence, but I suppose could have been in deference to Kaylee's spirit, I spoke to a man standing nearby. "Did you know her well?"

The man replied casually, "No, not really, you?"

No, I thought, *not really*, and I think I told him that, but I'm not sure, as the others began milling about, some cupping their hands around the wildflowers, holding them as one would hold a baby's cheeks and closing their eyes, touching the flower to their faces—*probably on drugs*, I thought—then thought about asking Doctor Henry for a handful of cannabis cookies—maybe some whiskey.

My conversation with the man yielded no information about Margery—he had not been here long and had only vaguely heard about "the bungee jumper"—little concrete information beyond that—or maybe I can't remember the details—but what seemed clear was his opinion of the town as a sort of mountain paradise, as I had thought briefly upon first arriving, despite, he said, its high mortality rate. Most people came here as an alternative to dying in the hot, congested lowlands, so their last view alive might ease the passage.

I pointed out that the feeling of hell in the form of hot, congested lowlands could accompany someone wherever they went, even in this pseudo-paradise, and that the mountains, at their extreme, could provide their own kind of special frozen hell.

"Oh," the man responded, "thanks for that. It's taken me months to claw my way out of that sort of ugly thinking."

He moved fast through the meadow, escaping my cynicism, leaving tromped upon wildflowers in his wake, bent over … slowly rising back to the sunlight.

A few people were talking with Doctor Henry—while Doctor Henry had some status, some power and influence, there was, as he had suggested, no real organizational power to this town—supplies came and went—and people died, occasionally replaced by others, but there was no system in place and I got the sense that everyone knew their town, their social experiment, their moment was no more than the flash of a lightning bug in the universe.

I felt bad. Defeated. But I still had a shred of hope—Margery.—If I could find her—literally or metaphorically, metaphor a poor substitute for physical reality—then maybe I could return to my original reality, the one I was dissatisfied with when I set off into the forest.

I waited forever for the others to finish telling Doctor Henry all about their ailments before approaching him. "Anything about Margery?" I asked.

"It's not uncommon for people to disappear."

"Yeah, but don't people magically come together for search parties?"

"Parties, yes, searching, yes, but seldom to search for other people."

"Except you," I said. "And me. So let's go."

Doctor Henry leveled his eyes at me, matter of fact, and said, "Where exactly?"

I suggested we hike along the stream to the confluence, searching for a body, so we could at least confirm Margery's death.

Doctor Henry looked at me again with pity, and said, quietly, "Lead the way. I'll follow."

We started below the cliff, and hiked through dense underbrush. We climbed over boulders and crags—Doctor Henry surprisingly nimble for a man clearly older than I was. We stopped and stared at fallen tree limbs that looked human in the water. By the time we'd crashed through underbrush onto a road where a narrow bridge led over the stream, leading onto a two-track snaking up a steep incline, the sun was well on its way west. We hiked the trail leading to the confluence, where we stood next to the ashes and the spent wood of the funeral pyre, gawking at a massive torrent gushing and boiling through the gorge—impossible to navigate—possibly Margery's final resting place.

How had her body traveled so far? If she had died on impact, wouldn't her body have gotten hung up on a limb or branch or something? Since apparently it hadn't, then maybe she had survived, maybe she was alive, broken but alive—in pain but reacting instinctively to stay afloat, until she would eventually drown in the gorge. None of those circumstances sounded good. Why hadn't my love been strong enough to pull her from the edge? Maybe because I never told her, but surely she had to know. Our connection was that strong. Maybe she did not love me enough. But that sort of thinking seemed childish. Do we really keep score cards on love?

I sat on the smooth stones that tailed to a point where the two streams connected to form the river crashing down the gorge. Doctor Henry sat next to me. We were in sunlight, but the shadows were approaching. My body ached and each thought about her came with the feeling of pounding water, of tumbling through the roaring current, being hurled and smashed against the rocks—one and then another. I turned to Doctor Henry, wanting him to save me again. He was a doctor, after all, albeit a strange one, a doctor who laughed at my love for Margery. Maybe he thought it immature, unbecoming someone of my—what? Experience? I would have to confront him, challenge his notion of love, but I was wary—maybe afraid his ridiculing laughter might reduce me to something less than human. More likely, however, I was afraid he would tell me the truth about Margery.

13

W E TALKED, OUR TONE CASUAL, but a little forced, at least for me, while I struggled to control what lurked beneath. We commented on the sheer beauty of the earth, the gushing water and the mercy of pleasant weather before Doctor Henry decided to ease my discomfort.

"She lived here about a year, maybe longer—I seem to recall her arriving in the spring, not like now."

During our conversation, I learned details about her past that shed only diffuse light on who she had been—artist, housewife, poet and accountant, mother and environmental activist—a full life—and an avid hiker, cross-country skier, and most recently daredevil of sorts, parachuting, rock climbing, and the bungee cord jumping.

I compared it to my own life—husband, teacher, father of two, estranged from wife, kids in late twenties pursuing their own lives—no grandkids—my own adventures in the wilderness, climbing mountains, my long solo journeys becoming more desperate. But our respective past lives bore little significance to the moment and what might have been.

Margery

Finally, as long, irregularly shaped shadows from the cliff touched my arm, I asked, as calmly as I could, "Why did you laugh?"

Doctor Henry shook his head. "I wasn't laughing at you."

"At what then? Love?"

"Of course not …"

"What then?"

"I was laughing at the irony … I suppose that was it … although that doesn't describe it adequately."

Time was hurrying past, part of me in the sun's warmth and the other part cooling in the shadow where Doctor Henry's voice seemed to echo out of darkness. "Margery couldn't love you," he said. "At least not in the way you wanted."

I glared at him and thought, *Come on, out with it, tell me now, I'm ready.*

"Physically," he said, his voice rising. "Not in the sense we talk about love, nothing carnal … nothing erotic, no physical connection that might have enhanced your … whatever you felt … I'm guessing something less earthbound."

I had braced myself for whatever might come and thought I was prepared.

"I treated her as best I could and even consulted her doctors …." He stared at the gorge—as if Margery's doctors lived there—while we both knew they could be anywhere, doctors in the very air looking, searching, working hard to manipulate our existence to eliminate suffering, some misguided, most not.

The smooth, oval stones were beginning to glow grayish pink and blue in the evening and I'd crossed into the shadows, joining Doctor Henry in the cool shade of Margery's cliff. We settled in comfortably, the smooth stones forming into a natural recliner, the air soft, and my sense of panic having eased, the physical world still kind to me, and perhaps allowing him to tell the truth without fear of killing the patient.

"She was diagnosed with metastasized stage four ovarian cancer."

Funny how I felt nothing extraordinary, only the comfort of the moment, the peace that sometimes comes with truth. I remember picking up a smooth gray-blue stone, rubbing it between my thumb and forefingers, and throwing it as far as I could into the turbulent water. Why didn't anyone tell me? Were they afraid I'd be like Josh and run away? I might have. I might have escaped this turmoil—but how would I have felt then? So that was it? That drove her to fling herself off a cliff? Something was missing, and I felt cheated. If I had been able to lie in her arms every night until she slipped away, I wouldn't have run. Maybe my love would have saved her. Maybe it would have convinced the cancer into remission. But, lingering in the cooling air at the confluence, there was more.

Doctor Henry glanced at me. "Early on, she had surgery … they didn't get it all, so she had another surgery. And another when it came back. She met it head on."

That was the part of Margery I felt I knew, her spirit, her will and determination. But it still didn't fully explain why she stopped fighting and decided to fly into the air without a bungee cord.

Doctor Henry had been measuring out information like someone giving radiation—a technician monitoring the patient after each dose.

"The surgeries were hard on her. The last one … the doctors made some mistakes."

"Like what?"

"They severed nerves … irreparably … she lost all sensation."

Suddenly the relative comfort of my surroundings turned oppressive and I shoved my fists into the smooth stones, muttering, "fuck," and I wanted to stand, but my body wouldn't respond, frozen in place, perhaps by panic, but still choosing to believe even now that I was exerting my own will, similar to Margery's.

Doctor Henry gave me an extra dose. "She couldn't feel anything."

No, that wasn't true; she felt something, I know she did. And now I didn't trust Doctor Henry. Did he know more but was unwilling to tell me? I took a deep breath, and had to know everything about Margery, no matter how painful. Bring on the pain. I loved her—unconditionally—and accepted all that came with it.

I stared at Doctor Henry. "I could have helped."

"Maybe," he replied. "In the short time she and I had together, we discussed neuroplasticity and the possibility of circumventing the damage, growing new neural pathways …"

"You did more than talk about it, didn't you?"

Margery

"We tried everything … including physical manipulation … lots of it, with me and someone else … although I think it was all a bit too methodical."

"This someone else?" I asked. "He left? Like you think I would have?"

"Yes, he left, but not like you or Josh."

I wanted to blame him, cuss him out—but was determined to end this discussion civilly, politely, scientifically. "So," I said, "maybe there was a component missing, something I could have provided."

"I think," Doctor Henry said, "it was a time issue. Eventually she might have recovered some feeling. With you, who knows, it might have worked … but I thought that about her and Kaylee too …"

What was he saying exactly, that Margery essentially had some sort of physical, maybe sexual, contact with everyone but me? Did I want to ask? Or had I enough of this truth telling? But the possible truth made some sense. Maybe Kaylee and Margery had a connection, something vastly different than what I imagined upon meeting Kaylee—the older person grasping at youth and destroying the young person in the process. Clearly, their relationship had been unique—they were bound together by suffering, sharing similar fates, and whatever affection they had for one another was at least reciprocal, if not pure. Did Josh know and did it matter? Ultimately, I didn't care—probably nobody else did either.

"She ran out of time," Doctor Henry said.

The implication was clear—Margery might regain only the faintest quiver of feeling in this earthly world, just enough to remember what it was like, only to lose the sensations a final time.

Doctor Henry told me all about Margery's bungee jumping, and from what I could decipher in his halting scientific description, her jumps made her feel alive, moments in the middle of the leap when everything felt glorious, all memory, all past and present packed into those moments, an immediacy she didn't get during her own psilocybin treatments. She had developed an exhilarating routine that she knew would end in her natural return to earth.

Could I assume she avoided my touch because it was too late? My feelings for her under "normal" circumstances might have resulted in, at the very least, an affair, like a meteor across the night sky, and at most, a steady burning desire and encapsulating love until one or both of us passed away.

"Like my Jackie," Doctor Henry said.

That was, at least subconsciously, what I'd come to expect with Margery, at least the chance to find out, the chance to ride the meteor or to experience what remained of our lives together. Now, of course, I would never know—I had only the brief time we'd spent together and my memory of what could have been.

So Doctor Henry's earlier laughter had revealed an even greater cynicism than my own, and I hoped it was not merely because he was older, because I would be there soon.

We sat until the moon rose over the eastern ridge and talked about everything that seemed meaningless—I watched the darkness of the long narrow gorge and imagined Margery there, not as a broken corpse but as a ghost—a phantasmagorical entity that I could at once feel and yet not—a woman I loved but could never merge with—unless perhaps …

No, I would leave in the morning, I would return from the wilderness as I had often done before, and play out my life in the valley below, at least until I needed to escape again—would Margery be with me then—would she always be with me?

A mosquito landed on my ear and I slapped at it, and then got up. Doctor Henry and I walked back to his house, picking up my backpack along the way.

"You should stay here tonight," he said. It wasn't a question or command. Probably just some need to verbalize an immediate plan, maybe to avoid the ubiquitous chaos. But standing with him inside didn't feel right. Doctor Henry suggested I try Margery's empty house. "As far as I know, no one's claimed it yet."

We said our goodbyes outside in the dark. I was leaving early in the morning, and didn't want to say goodbye again—parting invariably becomes awkward once properly accomplished—although he did politely suggest waking him if I had more questions. "Take care of that tooth," he said. And I was already down the dark road to Margery's when I heard him calling out, "You might also want a CT scan." The idea lingered, his words hanging in the air like a death threat.

I eased into Margery's house and felt her presence, a crushing spiritual embrace. No, I thought, I could not bear it any longer—I wasn't going to find her. Not here. I wasn't going to find peace in an empty house. I was not ready to fully understand or accept the gift she had given me, perhaps something akin to the psilocybin treatment—the courage to face the inevitable—her love forever suspended in the clean clear air of eternity—and I fled, heaving on my backpack, traipsing off into the night, up the road, thrashing through the dark woods, stumbling upon a footpath, and hiking in the moonlight, pushing past that big sloping rock slab, and gaining the crest of the ridge where a lone boulder glowed in the moonlight, climbing on top and, through the forest, the faint glimmering light from that strange town—into the glorious moonlit night, I cried, "Margery!"

If only I could hear her reply.

About the Author

Jeffrey Penn May has won several fiction awards, including one from *Writer's Digest*. He has received a Pushcart nomination and was a Landmark Prize finalist. Jeff wrote and performed a story for Washington University Radio and was a consultant to a St. Louis theater company.

Among other occupations, Jeff has been a waiter, hotel security officer, credit manager, deckhand, technical data engineer, and creative writing teacher. Jeff's adventures include floating a home-built raft from St. Louis to Memphis, navigating a John boat to New Orleans, digging for Pre-Columbian artifacts, and climbing mountains from Alaska to South America.

For more information about Jeff's world and works, visit *askwritefish.com*.

You Might Also Enjoy

CARNIVAL FARM
by Lisa Jacob

When a local veterinarian decides to take over a traveling carnival's petting zoo, she doesn't realize the insanity behind the scenes.

PIOUS REBEL
by Jory Post

After her partner dies suddenly, Lisa Hardrock realizes how little she knows about the life she's been living—and starts exploring her questions in a blog that unexpectedly goes viral.

STILL LIFE
by Paul Skenazy

When his wife, Edie, dies, Will Moran abandons all he used to be, and do, to paint still life canvases of rocks and driftwood on the walls of his house.

Available from Paper Angel Press in
hardcover, trade paperback, digital, and audio editions
paperangelpress.com

Manufactured by Amazon.ca
Acheson, AB